Escape from Big Muddy

Books by Eric Wilson

The Tom and Liz Austen Mysteries

Also available by Eric Wilson

Escape from Big Muddy

A Liz Austen Mystery

by

ERIC WILSON

HarperCollins*Publishers*Ltd

The author appreciates the kind assistance of Saskatchewan Tourism. Special thanks to Flo Connolly and Sadie Whitemoon, and to each person who has helped by commenting on early drafts.

As in his other mysteries, Eric Wilson writes here about imaginary people in a real landscape.

Find Eric Wilson at http://hypbus.com/ewilson/

http://www.harpercollins.com/canada

HarperCollins books may be purchased for educational, business, or sales promotional use. For information please write: Special Markets Department, HarperCollins Canada, 55 Avenue Road, Suite 2900, Toronto, Ontario M5R 3L2.

First published in hardcover by HarperCollins Publishers Ltd: 1997
First published in paperback by HarperCollins Publishers Ltd: 1998

Canadian Cataloguing in Publication Data

Wilson, Eric
   Escape from big muddy

(A Liz Austen mystery)
ISBN 0-00-648185-X

I. Title. II. Series: Wilson, Eric. A Liz Austen mystery.

PS8595.I583E82   jC813'.54   C97-931252-3
PZ7.W54Es

---

98 99 00 01 02 03 04 OPM 10 9 8 7 6 5 4 3 2 1

Printed and bound in the United States

cover design: Richard Bingham
cover and chapter illustrations: Richard Row
logo photograph: Lawrence McLagan

This book is dedicated with affection to my friend
Chris Patrick
and to the memory of master storyteller
Robert Louis Stevenson

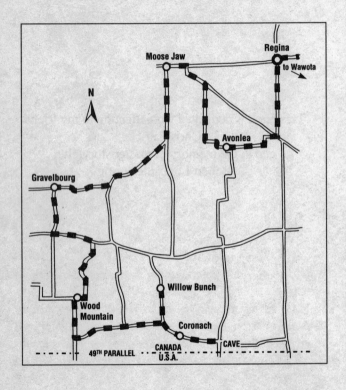

1

Elizabeth Kean Austen has an important decision to make.

With her fellow citizens, Liz is voting on the future of Canada's national parks. Should some parkland be sold to private developers to raise money for the government, or should parks be protected for the enjoyment of all people?

Using a computer in her home, Liz registers her vote. Within hours, Ottawa's powerful SuperBrain-987 computer will advise the News Channel what the voters have decided. Liz will certainly be tuning in for the result.

She presses a button on her keypad. A small plastic card emerges from the machine; it is her computer

democracy citizen card. Liz studies her holograph se-
curity image on the CDCC, then pops the card into her
electronic purse.

At age sixty, Liz Austen is a successful woman
whose hobbies include riding horses and collecting
books. She and her brother, Tom, are partners in
Austen Associates, Winnipeg's world-renowned private detective agency. They only investigate crimes
that involve children, such as kidnapping.

The computer buzzes. "INCOMING IMAGE," de-
clares a metallic voice. "ACCEPT OR DECLINE?"

"Caller's identity?" Liz inquires of the machine.

"NUMBER ONE FAN."

Liz smiles happily. "Put her through, please."

The face of Alice Leung appears instantly on the
Liquid\Screen that fills one wall of Liz's office.
Alice is a vivacious girl of twelve who makes peo-
ple feel good about life. "How nice of you to make
contact today," Liz says with delight. "What's new,
Alice?"

On the Liquid\Screen, the girl's dark eyes sparkle
with pleasure. "Guess what, Liz! I scored an A+ in
history on the School Channel. They loved my report
on the birth of the Internet."

"Congratulations, Alice. I'm so proud of you."

"Thanks, Liz. Listen—I've got a new project for the
Austen Channel. I'm hoping to give kids some brand-
new, never-before-told inside-info on your first case.
The one at Casa Loma—way back, before you started
wearing contact lenses."

"Actually, Alice, Casa Loma wasn't my first case.
Something happened before that."

The girl's mouth falls open. "What!?"

Liz smiles. "I've never told this story before, but I can't keep it a secret forever. I was reminded of the case when I recently visited my Aunt Melody, and she mentioned it. Shall I tell you what happened?"

"Yes, please! Wow—what a scoop!" Alice can be seen settling back comfortably on her Water\Chair. "What happened, Liz? I'm all ears!"

"Well, it all began a long time ago when I was twelve . . ."

* * *

It was a warm night in June. I was in a small Manitoba town; my aunt and I were travelling west by Greyhound, and the bus had stopped for a coffee break. It was three in the morning. The driver sat with a coffee in an all-night café, while I stood outside, looking in darkened store windows. It was exciting to be in a new place, and I was interested in everything.

Then I saw a man running.

He was reflected in the window of a store. He wore jeans and a T-shirt. In his hand was a book.

I'm telling you, the man looked terrified.

Then I heard a distant rumble in the darkness surrounding the town. The sound grew louder—the man ran faster, more desperately. Crossing the wide street, he reached the bus.

His black eyes stared into mine. Then he quickly climbed inside the Greyhound and disappeared from sight. Heart thumping, I looked into the distance—the noise had become the sound of motorcycles. They were moving fast, headlights cutting the darkness.

The bikers swept around a corner and roared in my direction. I stepped closer to the bus, ready to climb inside if necessary. Store windows reflected the jagged patterns of the bikers' headlights. They rode in a pack, men and women in leathers and boots, their motorcycles glittering with chrome. As they swept past, I saw tattooed shoulders and faces. There were a couple of Confederate flags on the bikes; the licence plates were from California.

I stared until the bikers were swallowed by the darkness. All that remained of their passage was the smell of dust in the air.

Quickly, I climbed into the bus. I couldn't see the man—he was hiding somewhere. I took the aisle seat beside my Aunt Melody, who was asleep. Looking into the coffee shop, I mentally urged the driver to *hurry up*! I kept checking the night for the bikers, fearful that they'd return.

At last, the driver finished his coffee and we left the town to its dreams. Pulling onto the Trans-Canada Highway, we continued the journey west towards Saskatchewan. But not for long, because suddenly the bus pulled over to the side of the empty highway. Looking in the mirror, the driver said, "Where did you come from?"

The man with the book had emerged from the tiny washroom at the back of the bus. His intense eyes stared from hollow sockets; he looked tired and unhealthy. Pulling out some American money, the man peeled off a bill.

"You're heading for Regina?"

The driver nodded. "We arrive there tomorrow morning."

"Gimme a one-way ticket to Regina."

"I'm not so sure . . ."

"Hey," the man said, "I'm not dangerous. Let me ride with you."

"Well . . . okay."

As the bus resumed its journey, the man came down the aisle to sit in the empty seat across from me. On his T-shirt were a skull and the faded words *Born to Die*. On his shoulder, a tattoo showed a body hanging from a gallows noose.

I noticed a couple of the bus passengers staring at the man, and others whispering together. I guess he looked scary with his ripped jeans and dusty motorcycle boots, but all I felt was curiosity. Who was this guy?

The only thing he carried was that book. I glanced at the title: *The Secret of Happiness*. "Sir!" I kept my voice low, not wanting to disturb Aunt Melody's sleep. "What's your name?"

The man glanced at me. "Billy Bones."

"I really love reading. Could I borrow your book?"

Glancing at *The Secret of Happiness*, Billy Bones shook his head. "Nobody touches this book. It's all I've got." He sighed unhappily.

"Are you okay? Do you need help?"

A brief smile flickered across his face. "I'm okay, kid. But thanks for asking." He sighed again, then looked at me. "What's your name?"

"Liz Austen."

"You remind me of my sister, when we were kids. How old are you, Liz?"

"I'm twelve. My aunt's treating me to a vacation in Saskatchewan." I showed him a brochure for Benbow Farm, the first destination on our holiday. "They've got horseback riding and everything!"

"It looks nice," Billy Bones said, studying the brochure. "Maybe a guy could take shelter there, and get his energy back."

"Are you in trouble, Mr. Bones?"

"You bet I am. But I'll survive—I always do."

"Why were those bikers chasing you?"

My aunt opened her sleepy eyes. "Liz, you should get some sleep."

I whispered good night to Billy Bones. "We'll talk again in the morning," I promised him.

Closing my eyes, I thought about the bikers and Billy Bones. Truth to tell, I'd expected a fairly predictable vacation with my fairly predictable aunt. But already there'd been excitement and a mysterious stranger—things looked promising!

Eventually, I drifted off to sleep. When I awoke, my body was stiff, and sunshine was on my face. Aunt Melody was studying one of her textbooks; there was no sign of Billy Bones.

Yawning, I put on my glasses. As I did, the bus braked to a stop. We were in the middle of the open prairie. At the side of the road, a man had signalled the Greyhound to pull over; he wore faded jeans and a leather jacket. Close by, I saw a Harley-Davidson motorcycle.

As the biker stepped into the bus, I looked out the window at a nearby hillside. Watching from the top was a gang of bikers—they looked like the ones I'd seen chasing Billy Bones!

I glanced swiftly at the washroom. The door was closed; a sign read OCCUPIED.

"I'm looking for someone," the biker said. Ignoring the driver's protest, he walked down the aisle searching faces. People looked scared; my skin was damp with sudden sweat. Taking my hand, Aunt Melody said, "Don't worry, Liz. I'm sure we're perfectly safe."

The man looked at me with cold eyes. There was a white scar across his face, as if he'd been in a knife fight. A tattoo of a spider's web covered his shaved head and his neck. The tattoo included a tarantula; the hairy black spider seemed to lurk behind the biker's ear. On the back of his leather jacket was a cruel face and the words *Death Machine*.

As I tightly squeezed my aunt's hand, the biker approached the washroom. Then the sign changed to VACANT and the door slowly opened.

2

I was so afraid—I expected violence at any moment. But, to my astonishment, out of the washroom stepped an elderly man, leaning on a cane.

Was this brilliant acting by Billy Bones? I stared at the man—no, impossible.

The biker concluded his search and left the bus. As the Greyhound picked up speed, I quickly told my aunt about the bikers chasing Billy Bones. "He's got something they want, Aunt Melody! I bet it's a treasure map or something."

She smiled. "You and your brother, what imaginations you've got! You see mysteries everywhere."

"One day we'll be famous detectives, Aunt Melody. Wait and see."

"When I was a girl, I loved Nancy Drew mysteries." Aunt Melody stood up. "I'm going to ask the driver about the enigmatic Mr. Bones."

I went with her. Through the bug-splattered windshield, I saw the wide-open prairie. In the enormous blue sky, a hawk hovered, searching for its next meal.

The driver glanced at us. He was wearing silver shades—I couldn't see his eyes. "Yes, folks?"

"Last night," my aunt said, "a man purchased a ticket to Regina, using American money. We haven't reached Regina, but he's no longer on the bus. Why?"

"I don't know, lady. I left him at Elkhorn, while you and the kid were sleeping."

"But why did he get off early?"

The driver shrugged. "Just as well he did. That was one tough dude looking for him, and did you see his biker pals? Big, big trouble." He pointed at a highway sign. "Moosomin's next. You'd better gather your belongings."

Back at my seat, I made a horrified discovery. "Aunt Melody," I exclaimed. "I've been robbed!"

*   *   *

My aunt was shocked. "Is your money gone?"

"No, but I'm missing the brochure for Benbow Farm. I bet Billy Bones took it!"

The bus was slowing down. "Hurry, Liz," my aunt said, "we're almost there."

We stepped from the Greyhound into powerful heat. Bright sunshine reflected from the windows of the Moosomin coffee shop that doubled as a bus station.

People inside were sipping drinks filled with ice cubes.

An older man was waiting to shake hands with us. "I'm Mr. Husband," he said with a smile, "but please call me George. My wife Doris and I are your hosts at Benbow Farm. Hot enough for you?"

"It's surprising for June," Aunt Melody replied.

"There'll be a wind tonight. It'll keep the mosquitoes down. We'll play some softball in the yard."

Aunt Melody shook her head. "Tonight, I'll be studying in my bedroom. I'm a university student, George, taking opera, and I've got major exams in exactly one month. With all this studying, I'm worried Liz may get bored."

"She'll find lots to do," George promised.

"Benbow Farm is an unusual name," I said to him. "It reminds me of Jim Hawkins and the Admiral Benbow Inn."

"You're right—my wife and I are great fans of *Treasure Island*." Mr. Husband lifted our gear into the trunk of his big car. "My friends are all retired," he told us, "and living in rest homes in Wawota. I see them walking for exercise. I get my exercise by still running the farm."

Aunt Melody sat in the back. As we drove through the pleasantly shaded streets of Moosomin, I looked at Mr. Husband. "You raise Arabian horses, right? I've never been riding before—will I get a chance?"

"You bet!"

George's blue eyes were friendly; his skin was weathered by the storms of many years. During the long drive across the prairie, he discussed the sights, such as a gigantic new grain elevator under construction.

"Harvested crops are stored in those," he said, "then

taken to market by railroad." George pointed at a deserted house alone on a hill. The wood was black, the windows smashed. "You'll see a lot of abandoned buildings on your travels. These days, a person needs a really big farm to compete with the corporations. It's tough."

*   *   *

Eventually, we approached Benbow Farm. It was set in a landscape of rolling hills with lots of trees. "Saskatchewan is known for wheat and grain," Mr. Husband explained, "but this area is mostly cattle country. My father homesteaded here, and the land is still in the family. In addition to the Arabians, we also raise Aberdeen Angus cattle."

We'd been travelling on a local highway with little traffic. Now, we turned onto a long dirt road. A wooden fence stretched along its side, all the way to a distant house. "I see the fence needs work," George commented. "There's always something new in my job jar."

At the end of the long, long driveway, we stopped at the Husbands' house. Nearby was a barn and various large sheds containing farm equipment. George's wife, Doris, smiled as we stepped from the car. "Welcome to Benbow," she said, hugging us both. "Please consider yourselves family."

"It's great to be here," I said.

"Come meet our neighbours. They drove over to welcome you."

We met a nice woman and her young son and daughter, who were feeding grass to a horse named Comet. Then I met Tammy, the world's friendliest Alsatian.

"What a sweetie," I said, stroking Tammy's soft ears.

"How was your winter in Manitoba?" Doris asked.

"Brutal."

"Same here. Wawota means *deep snow* and we really lived up to our name!"

George lifted our luggage out of the car. "We'll take the suitcases to your room," he said, "and then go feed the cattle."

Inside the house, one long room combined a kitchen, dining room, and living room. George and Doris proudly showed us pictures of their eleven grandchildren, and a bunch of trophies they'd won for their Arabians.

Aunt Melody and I unpacked in our room; the window framed a beautiful view of a nearby hill. Back outside, we stood chatting with George and Doris in the sunshine. I watched a hummingbird at a feeder—wings a speedy blur—then saw a car stop at the distant secondary highway.

A man got out. He waved a thank you to the driver, and watched the car pull away. Then he began walking along the driveway towards the farm. At first, he was too distant to recognize, but as he got steadily closer, I saw that he carried a book.

"Aunt Melody," I cried. "It's Billy Bones!"

* * *

Looking hot, dusty, and tired, Billy Bones handed me the Benbow Farm brochure. "This is yours, Liz. Thanks for the loan."

I introduced him to the others and then asked, "How'd you get here, Mr. Bones?"

"I hitched some rides. Saskatchewan people are friendly." He turned to the Husbands. "What's the size of this spread?"

"Twelve hundred acres," George replied.

"Got a high spot of land?"

"Yup."

"You're a vacation farm, right? Got a room for me?"

George shook his head. "There's a basement room, but I'm afraid we already have guests. I'm sure they wish to have their holiday here alone. Perhaps another time?"

Billy Bones turned to my aunt with pleading in his hollow eyes. "Please, miss, let me stay. I'm so tired, I just need a place to rest."

"Well . . . "

I looked at her. "Please say yes, Aunt Melody."

She smiled. "Okay. I'm sure there's lots of room for all of us on twelve hundred acres!"

"Then it's settled." George turned to Billy Bones. "You can stay in the basement room."

"Great!" Pulling out his American money, Billy Bones handed several bills to George. "Let me know when I've used that up. Now, where's that high point of land? Could you take me there?"

"Come with us—we're going to feed the cattle."

"I'll stay here." Aunt Melody smiled at Doris. "We can get acquainted."

I opened the passenger door of the farm's battered pickup; pictured on the door was an Aberdeen Angus. As I climbed inside, Billy Bones got into the back of the truck.

"I'll ride here," he said to George. "I need some fresh air."

After a short drive, we turned onto a gravel road. The trees were so pretty, sprouting their new leaves. Ducks flew up from a pond that reflected the blue of the sky. "See the beaver house?" George said, pointing. "They blocked the pipe that carries water under this road, so the highway department had to dynamite the pipe clear." He laughed. "But those beavers blocked it again."

I glanced through the rear window. "Billy Bones just popped a pill."

"Maybe he suffers from headaches." George looked in the rearview mirror. "What's that book he's holding?"

"It's called *The Secret of Happiness*." I studied the sad face of Billy Bones. "I guess it hasn't worked for this guy."

"Doris is a wonderful cook—he'll cheer up fast."

"What's your favourite thing about farming?" I asked.

"I suppose it's being with the livestock. When I was a young fellow, I loved riding my horse between our farm and the school. We had one teacher for all the grades. I must show you the cairn where our schoolhouse used to be."

George turned into a field; the truck followed a bumpy path towards cattle patiently awaiting their meal. We got out of the cab, and Billy Bones jumped down from the back. "These are yearling heifers," George explained. "They're descended from Aberdeen Angus cattle imported from Scotland. These days, our stock is being exported to Scotland. All things change—that's one thing I've learned."

George and Billy Bones hefted big yellow drums of feed over to the wooden trough. "Oats and barley," George said. "The feed supplements their diet until they can get enough grass."

Suddenly, Billy Bones dropped to his knees, clutching at his chest. As I ran to him, he fumbled in a pocket for his pills and swallowed two. "I'll be okay," he gasped.

Slowly, some colour returned to his face, but he stood up shakily, leaning on my shoulder for support. "Thanks, kid."

"What's wrong?"

Billy Bones shrugged, looking embarrassed. "My heart's a bit weak—I take this medication for it. I guess I was stupid to lift that drum."

"I'm sorry," George said.

Billy Bones waved a hand. "Don't worry about it, Pops. Stress is what's eating me alive."

As Mr. Husband returned to his work, Billy Bones stared into space. "Never cross the brotherhood. I did, and it was my biggest mistake."

"What do you mean?"

"My life's been tough, Liz. I know everything about computers, but I never fit in anywhere. My mother is very wealthy. She was good to me but I didn't care. Her gifts couldn't change me. I ran away to the streets. Mother wasn't pleased, especially because I took someone with me."

"Who?"

"Two of my mother's servants are married. Their daughter grew up in my home. On her sixteenth birthday, she ran away with me. I thought she loved me, but I was wrong. She only loved the danger of the streets."

Billy Bones sighed. "We were together for a few years. Then she convinced me to join a biker gang with her. That was the beginning of the end for us. Eventually, she left me for another man."

For long moments, Billy Bones said nothing. Then he glanced at me with sad eyes.

"We both stayed with the gang. I was into chemicals, and my habit kept growing. I needed money for drugs—lots of money. She suggested we rip off my wealthy mother. I fought the idea, but I was weak." Billy Bones looked troubled. "Liz, I stole from my mother. It fills me with shame."

I was so amazed that I didn't know what to say. His story was stranger than any book I'd ever read!

Before Billy Bones could say anything more, George called over to us. "I'm all finished. Let's go see that high point of land."

*   *   *

After seeing the hill, Billy Bones asked George an unusual question. "Is it okay if I visit the local cemetery?"

"Sure thing, but why?"

Billy Bones shrugged. "I feel peaceful in cemeteries. I like reading the tombstones, guessing at the people's lives." He climbed into the back of the pickup. "Would you mind taking me?"

"Not at all."

We drove along a series of gravel roads, enjoying the sunshine on the trees and fields. A hawk soared above, and it was exciting to see a coyote bounding across an enormous green field.

"Ever seen a twister?" I asked.

George shook his head. "I never want to. Down south in the badlands, they get a twister that folks call the Big Muddy Express. There was a special on TV last year about all the damage."

George stopped the pickup beside a hedge. "The cemetery's this way," he said, leading us around the bushes. "It's behind all these trees."

Birds twittered in the sunshine and the grass was a vivid green. One grave we looked at was amazing. It was protected by a stone angel, taller than I was. The white marble of her wings had darkened over the decades, but her face was beautiful—sweet and kind.

"Years ago," said George, "a local woman died. Her husband wanted a special way to celebrate her life, so he purchased this statue. It came all the way from Italy, by boat and train. More than a thousand dollars he paid—a lot of money then."

The tombstone inscription ended with *Good night dear heart, good night, good night.* "Sad, don't you think?" George said. "After that, the poor fellow went out of his mind. They put him in the mental institution."

"They're both buried here," Billy Bones said, reading the headstone. "She died in 1919, and he went in 1943. They waited a long time for their reunion." He looked around at the peaceful scene. "Maybe I'll wait a long time, too, but I'll be with my sweet one again."

He turned to George. "This is a beautiful place. Thanks for bringing me, Mr. Husband."

* * *

Back at the farm, Billy Bones went inside. George offered to show Aunt Melody and me the barn, which was really large. "We hauled a hundred loads of fieldstone to build the foundation," he explained, pausing beside a tractor.

The barn had the sweet smell of hay and bedding straw. On the far wall, a door was open to the paddock. The field was enclosed by fences; inside the paddock, horses played in the sunshine.

"That bay stallion is named Khaaleb," George said. "One day in the barn, I found Khaaleb lying down, which is unusual for a horse. I thought he was sick, but then I discovered our cat had given birth. Khaaleb was having a close look at the newborn kittens." He chuckled. "Cute, eh?"

We ate a delicious supper, then George and I tossed a softball in the big front yard. As we did, Billy Bones prowled restlessly, constantly watching the horizon. Later, Doris and I enjoyed hot chocolate and a scrumptious puffed wheat cake. Aunt Melody worked in the bedroom on her opera notes, then joined us for the news on TV.

"Everyone's talking about that golden statue," Doris said. "I wonder where it is?"

"I'm sorry," Aunt Melody said. "You'll think me clueless, but what statue?"

I grinned at Doris. "My aunt is studying for her final exams at opera school, Mrs. Husband. She isn't paying attention to much else at the moment." I reached for a copy of *Maclean's* magazine. The cover showed a glamorous movie star holding an exquisite golden statue. "This statue is called the Sacred Egyptian Cat," I told Aunt Melody. "The woman is Winter Leigh."

"The movie star?"

I nodded, relieved to discover that my aunt knew *something* about real life. "See the jewels on the cat's collar? They alone are worth millions upon millions."

Doris nodded. "Not only that, but the statue is solid gold."

My aunt's eyebrows rose. "Wow—that's amazing. How did it get stolen?"

"Winter Leigh kept the golden statue on display in her mansion, which has a state-of-the-art computer alarm system. Even so, the Sacred Egyptian Cat disappeared."

"The cops suspect bikers," I told my aunt. "Motorcycles were seen in the neighbourhood the night of the robbery."

Doris turned up the TV volume. "The news is starting."

The famous missing statue was the lead story. Winter Leigh was seen outside her mansion—surrounded by microphones and cameras—as the news anchor excitedly told us the latest. "The superstar has offered a huge reward for the return of her sacred golden cat," he said as the report concluded. "Will she ever see it again? Stay tuned!"

Aunt Melody smiled at me. "You want to be a detective, right? Here's your chance—find the golden statue."

"Wouldn't that be great?"

"If Nancy Drew can do it, why not Liz Austen?"

When the news ended, Doris clicked off the television. "Winter Leigh has beautiful eyes." She nodded at my aunt. "So do you, Melody. You should star in movies."

"You're very kind, Doris, but opera's all I care about. I'm determined to succeed."

"What gives you such strength of mind?"

"I watched my younger brother fight cancer and win. To me, he's a hero. To overcome cancer—that proves anything can be achieved."

"You're studying voice?"

Aunt Melody nodded. "Plus the history of music, and the economics of managing an opera house." She smiled a bit ruefully. "My head is swimming with information—I've got exams in a month. But I wanted a holiday with my favourite niece, and June was the only possible month."

Doris sipped hot chocolate. "Next you're going to Regina?"

"Yes," Aunt Melody replied. "My distant cousin, Squire, has invited us to visit."

"You must see the IMAX movie show. The screen is five storeys high."

"We're going," I exclaimed happily. "Squire's promised us tickets."

In the kitchen, the computer beeped. "Incoming fax," Doris said, looking at the screen. "It's a reservation, from British Columbia. Callaghan O'Connor is coming with his family in two weeks. It'll be good to see them again."

I went outside in search of George, who was repairing the tractor. The light was almost gone from the sky; the land was dark. Frogs croaked their songs of love, and the wind moaned in my ears. Far in the distance, an orange light glowed at someone's farm; close by, I saw the silhouette of the barn. In the sky, dusky blue faded down to the horizon's dark pink.

George and Tammy joined me. As I patted the dog,

I said to George, "Where's Billy Bones?"

"He walked to the top of Spyglass Hill. That fellow likes to be where the land is high. He's a strange one, that Billy Bones."

3

In the morning, I awoke to the wind stirring the trees. For breakfast, we had delicious oatmeal with raisins and flax, then toast heaped with sweet strawberry preserves. "My tastebuds are applauding every bite," I told Doris. "Your cooking is so toothsome."

"That's a good word!" She turned to Aunt Melody. "Did you notice the frogs last night? That sound always sends me straight to sleep."

"Where's Billy Bones?" I asked George.

"He's waiting outside for Doris and me. He wants to see the old Halstat place, so we're dropping him there. Then we're going shopping in town."

Aunt Melody's eyes lit up. "Shopping? May we join you?"

Doris laughed. "Of course."

As we went outside, I looked at George. "What's the old Halstat place?"

"Doris and I were children during the Depression. Many people had nothing, and travelled the country looking for work or somewhere to live. The Halstats arrived from the east, with all their earthly possessions in a wagon box pulled by a team of skinny old horses. Mother and father, and eight kids. Built a house hidden among the trees, and there they lived."

Doris shook her head sadly. "They could only afford presentable clothes for half the kids, so the children took turns attending school. The parents didn't want to be on welfare, but there was no work."

"It was a loving family," George added, "and the kids turned out well. Grew up to be leaders, every one of them. The eldest son returned recently, for a visit. Said he remembered how kind people were to his family."

During the drive, I asked Billy Bones why he was interested in the Halstat house. "I dunno," he replied, "but it sounds like my kind of place. Real lonely."

"Aunt Melody," I said, "aren't you curious to see the Halstat place? Maybe we could shop another day."

Aunt Melody hesitated, then nodded. "Okay, Liz. Today's your turn to choose what we do. Tomorrow, I decide, and we'll be shopping for sure."

"Even if it's just the Shopping Channel," Doris said with a smile.

Soon after, George stopped at the side of the road. "The Halstat place is hidden among those trees. You'll have to walk home after, but it's not too far."

As we got out, Doris said, "Goodbye! Enjoy your morning."

Putting the car in gear, George gave us a wave. "We'll be home by this evening. Liz, don't forget we're going horseback riding tomorrow."

"Don't worry about that!"

"Well, goodbye then."

As they drove away, I shivered. "That was a bad omen, Aunt Melody. People should never say goodbye twice. Not that I'm superstitious, but I wish I'd brought my lucky penny."

We followed Billy Bones along a trail. "I love lilacs," Aunt Melody said, sniffing some blossoms. "I wonder if the Halstats planted these."

"This place really seems isolated," I commented. "I can't hear anything but the wind. The long winters must have been terrible for them."

Billy Bones pointed at the weathered walls of an old house, visible among the trees. "There it is."

My aunt took a picture of the small house, which was made of logs. It tilted to the side, looking ready to fall. "See the dried mud between the logs?" she said. "That's how they insulated their home."

The inside was a mess, so we didn't go in. Aunt Melody snapped another picture, then surprised me by taking one of Billy Bones holding his book. I wondered if he'd object, but he said nothing.

"When we get back to Benbow Farm," Aunt Melody said, "let's have some lunch."

We followed Billy Bones past the bushes to the gravel road. In every direction were green fields fringed by trees; there wasn't a car or house or person in sight. It was lonely, and it was beautiful.

We set out walking. The sun fried us, so I was glad I'd used sunscreen. I could tell Billy Bones wasn't enjoying himself; sweat poured down his grey face, and he popped another pill. He looked super stressed.

Suddenly, Billy Bones motioned for quiet. Eyes narrowed, he focused on the horizon. "Look!" A cloud of dust rose into the air, and I heard a roaring sound.

"The Death Machine," Billy Bones groaned. "They've tracked me down."

*   *   *

Hidden on a hill overlooking Benbow Farm, we looked down at the house. A motorcycle stood beside it and two people were at the door. One was a woman with blonde hair that looked bleached; the other was a man wearing sunglasses. "Blind Pew," Billy Bones whispered to himself. "He's found me—I never had a chance."

Blind Pew was scary, even from a distance. He wore a black T-shirt, jeans, and motorcycle boots. Instead of a helmet, he wore a small leather cap.

He dropped something beside the door. The woman guided him to the motorcycle and they roared away from the farm. Other bikers were waiting for them at the local highway. Soon they all disappeared into the distance.

Billy Bones raced down the hill, followed by Aunt Melody and me. At the house, he fell to his knees on the front porch. With desperate fingers, he snatched up a small, round piece of paper. It was dark on one side.

"The Black Spot," Billy Bones moaned. Hands trembling, he turned it over—someone had scrawled, *You have till ten tonight*.

"Ten o'clock," Billy Bones said, staggering to his feet. "Enough time—I can win yet. They won't get it from me."

"I'm calling 911," Aunt Melody declared.

As she hurried inside, I stared at Billy Bones. Sweat beaded his forehead and his skin was pale grey. He seemed to be in great pain. Then, suddenly, he grabbed my arm. "Liz, the password . . . is . . . NOEL. Remember it!" He groaned in misery. "Take my book to . . . "

Billy Bones stared at me. "Find . . . find my . . . " His eyes burned into mine. "Tell her . . . Dief died . . . in . . . "

He clutched a hand to his throat and swayed back and forth. A strange sound came from his mouth. Then he fell straight forward.

Horrified, I raced inside to get Aunt Melody. She stood at the computer. "I've contacted the Mounties," she said, then pressed a button. "A fax just arrived from Squire. I'm printing it out."

Grabbing her, I pointed at the porch. "Billy Bones! Quick, I think he's dead."

We ran to the porch. Aunt Melody tried desperately to revive Billy Bones, but it was no use. I burst into tears.

Aunt Melody hugged me and soothed me. We both cried for a bit, then mopped our eyes. "Aunt Melody, what should we do?"

"Liz, look!"

Dust rose on a distant road. Sunlight reflected off chrome. "It's the bikers," I gasped, "heading this way. But it's not ten o'clock."

"They lied," Aunt Melody said. "We've got to hide! Quick, to the barn!"

"Wait just a second." Kneeling beside Billy Bones, I took the book from his hand. It was creepy to do, but I forced myself. I had to read *The Secret of Happiness* and understand more about Billy Bones.

"Liz, hurry!"

The barn was close by. Racing across the yard, we ran into the cool interior. There were no animals inside the barn—I could see the horses through the open door in the far wall, safe in their large, sunny paddock. "The tractor," Aunt Melody cried. We crawled into the shadows behind the machine, which smelled of fuel. The barn creaked as the wind moaned through the rafters far above.

I leaned around the tractor to watch as the bikers arrived in clouds of dust. It was the same gang I'd first seen in the Manitoba town. The scariest was the guy with the spider's web tattoo. I shivered. A vein throbbed in my throat. Aunt Melody squeezed my hand. "We'll be okay, Liz," she whispered.

The two bikers who had delivered the Black Spot warning sat together on a big Harley-Davidson. The woman wore sunglasses; her bleached blonde hair was short-cropped, and she was dressed totally in black leather. Numerous earrings and studs glittered in the sunshine.

She ran to the porch. "Billy's dead," she cried. "Pew, he's dead!"

The man in sunglasses cursed. "Search him, you useless fool."

Moments later, she called, "Nothing!"

Again, Pew swore angrily. "Tarantula and the rest of you—try the house."

Several bikers ran inside. I heard crashing sounds that made me shiver with fear. A window was thrown open with such force that the glass broke, tinkling to the ground outside. The biker called Tarantula leaned out.

"Nothing here."

Blind Pew spat on the ground, swearing loudly. "You fools, you fools!"

The woman with the blonde hair turned to him. "You're the fool, Pew. It was your ridiculous idea to give Billy the Black Spot. We should have attacked without warning."

Pew's lip curled. "Question me again, and you die."

"Nobody threatens me," the woman replied in a cold and ominous tone.

Pew slammed his hand against the Harley. "Billy Bones hid on this farm," he yelled to the others. "I want revenge—torch the barn. Do it now!"

Running to a storage shed, Tarantula grabbed a gasoline canister and headed for the barn. I stared at Aunt Melody, frightened beyond belief. Dashing to the opposite side of the barn, we ran through the open door into the paddock. Sunshine struck my face.

"I don't think we were seen," Aunt Melody breathed, as we scurried along the wall of the barn. From inside we heard the cries of the bikers, followed by a *whooooosh* of sound. "The hay's on fire," Aunt Melody said. "Run, fast!"

"What about the horses?"

"They're safe from the fire—the paddock's really big."

Climbing over a fence, we left the paddock behind.

"We've got to reach the highway," Aunt Melody whispered, "and flag down a passing car."

Keeping low, we dashed to the shelter of the bushes that bordered the fence beside the farm driveway. We crawled along the fence for several minutes, then paused for breath. Through the bushes, I could see the house and garage. The bikers stood together near a shed, laughing as fire consumed the barn. The light of the savage orange flames glittered on their motorcycles.

Suddenly, the blonde biker ran to the largest shed. Looking in the open door, she yelled, "Someone bring Blind Pew here. Quick!"

Tarantula grabbed his arm and they hurried to the shed. "What is it?" Pew demanded. "What's going on?"

"Big trouble," the woman replied. "Quick, give me your gun. Someone's in here."

"Kill him!" Reaching inside his leather jacket, Blind Pew produced a silver handgun. "Do it—now!"

"Come with me." The woman took the gun from Blind Pew, and led him into the dark shed. They disappeared from sight; moments later, there was a flash of red-orange light, followed by a blast of sound.

The woman emerged from the shed with the smoking gun in her hand. Nearby, fire roared through the barn. The bikers gathered around her, staring. "Blind Pew is dead," she said, calmly lighting a cigarette. "I'm taking over."

She leapt onto the Harley and gunned the engine. The others ran to their bikes. The air was blasted by thundering engines as the gang raced past us, escaping the scene.

I turned to my aunt. "Holy Hannah! I can't believe what just happened!"

* * *

Soon after, a police car skidded to a stop. As officers jumped out, we ran to them.

"Thank goodness you're here," Aunt Melody cried. "Two men are dead!"

As more police cars arrived, George and Doris returned from their shopping expedition. They were horrified to learn of our ordeal, and shocked to see the barn destroyed and their home vandalized. We gave statements to the police, then sadly packed our luggage. With all the damage to the farm we couldn't continue our vacation.

"At least the horses are safe," I said to Aunt Melody, "even if I never got to ride one."

After sad farewells with the Husbands, we climbed into a police car. The Mounties had offered to drop us at the bus station in Moosomin—where we'd be catching the Greyhound to Regina—and we made the long drive listening to messages on their radio about the events at Benbow Farm.

Inside the bus, I slumped down in my seat, suddenly exhausted. "I was planning to read *The Secret of Happiness* on the bus, but now I'm too tired."

"Where is it?"

"In my backpack. Aunt Melody, we've landed in the middle of a major mystery—will Tom ever be jealous!"

"What's your theory?"

"Those bikers travelled all the way from California. Billy Bones must have stolen something important from them—a fortune in jewels or something like that."

Aunt Melody's eyes grew solemn. "Well, it's all over now. Poor Mr. Bones is dead, and so is the leader of the Death Machine."

"Their *former* leader is dead," I pointed out, "but they have a new leader now—that blonde woman. She was so scary."

"You're right." Aunt Melody shivered. "I wonder . . . No, I don't think . . . "

"What is it?" I asked anxiously. "What's wrong?"

Aunt Melody frowned. "Probably this shouldn't bother me, but those bikers could follow us to Regina. Remember the fax that arrived at the farm from my cousin, giving his address and phone number? Well, the fax was still on the machine when the bikers were trashing the house."

"So they could have seen it?"

Aunt Melody nodded. "But probably there's nothing to worry about."

"I'm sure you're right, Aunt Melody. We'll never see those bikers again."

4

When I woke up, it was morning. Ahead of the Greyhound was the strange sight of glass towers rising slowly out of the prairie. "We're approaching Regina," Aunt Melody said. "Aren't those skyscrapers beautiful?"

Entering the city, we saw kids skipping rope, watched over by grandparents who chatted on porches. Our bus passed a sign showing a red-coated Mountie welcoming us to the home town of the Royal Canadian Mounted Police. WELCOME, said the sign. *BIENVENUE*.

I turned to my aunt. "I can't wait to tour the RCMP training grounds. That's where Gramps got his start as a Mountie."

"I hope Squire remembers to meet us at the bus station. I did phone him to say we'd left the farm early, but he can be unreliable."

"What's Squire like?"

"He's my dad's cousin, so it's a distant relationship. Squire is fifty years old. He lives in Regina by himself in a nice house. Squire has rarely held a job, but he maintains a good lifestyle."

"Where does he get money?"

"Some people find Squire charming. I understand that every bit of his fancy clothing was a gift from some adoring, wealthy woman. He meets them on cruise ships."

"What do you think of him, Aunt Melody?"

"I haven't seen Squire for years, but I remember his sense of humour. Hey, there's Squire now!"

As the Greyhound pulled to a stop at the Regina bus depot, I saw a man waving to us. He had big ears, a big nose, and a big smile. Squire's black eyebrows jumped with every twitch of his big face. A red stone flashed on his ring finger; he clutched a bouquet of flowers, and wore a nametag with the words *Hi! I'm Squire*.

Squire presented the flowers to us and then hugged Aunt Melody. "You're much more beautiful than your pictures—get a new photographer!" He turned to me. "Another pretty relative. I'm a lucky man."

Squire picked up Aunt Melody's suitcase. "We'll get a cab."

"Did you hear what happened at Benbow Farm?" I asked.

He nodded. "Melody told me, when she phoned to

say you'd be arriving early. Scoundrels like those motorcycle riders should be locked away."

We loaded our things into a taxi. The friendly driver
had lived in Regina all her life. As we drove through the
city, she said, "All these beautiful trees were planted by pioneers, back when this place was called Pile O' Bones."

"Unusual name," Aunt Melody commented.

"Millions of buffalo once roamed the prairies. They
were hunted for their magnificent coats, and their
meat. The Native peoples used everything but the
bones. Those got piled here, along the banks of the
Wascana."

"I heard that Regina means *Queen* in Latin," I said.
"Is that right?"

She nodded. "The city was named in honour of
Queen Victoria. She ruled England when the British
controlled much of the world, including Canada. Red-
coated soldiers came from England and marched west
to the prairies to uphold the law. People respected
them. Thanks to those original Mounties, things were
pretty peaceful in the Canadian part of the Wild West."

When we arrived at Squire's house, he handed a
gold Visa card to the driver. "This card isn't valid," she
said, pointing at the expiration date.

"Oh, my goodness. You're right, and I don't have
any cash." Squire turned to Aunt Melody. "Would you
cover it, please? I'll pay you back—and that's a
promise."

"Certainly," Aunt Melody replied, reaching for her
wallet.

Getting out of the cab, I looked at the house. "Nice
place, eh?" Squire said. "It was designed in 1927 by

Francis Portnall himself." He pointed at the gable. "Look at the diamond-shaped detailing, all done with glass from bottles. Everyone is impressed by that."

He slapped my aunt's back. "Come inside! *Mi casa, su casa*. My house is your house."

"You speak Spanish?" I asked.

"Sure! I've learned plenty, lying on the beach in Mexico. It's a great place for a holiday, especially during our cold winters."

Inside, it was a nice old-fashioned home. The floors were solid oak, and there was a fireplace in the living room. In a corner was a work station with the latest in computers. Perched on the monitor were yellow flowers and a picture of Squire.

"You live alone?" I asked. "Doesn't it get lonely?"

"Not a chance—life's too interesting. I've only got one regret."

"What's that?"

"Not enough money." Squire shook his big head. "It's a tragedy, really. But one of these days, I'll hit the jackpot."

* * *

That afternoon, Aunt Melody and I visited the training facilities of the Royal Canadian Mounted Police. The place was like a small town. There were houses for the officers and barracks for the recruits, plus a gym, a pool, and even a beautiful little chapel. We had fun watching the young recruits, who saluted passing officers while marching smartly between the buildings where they trained.

"I keep thinking about Gramps," I said. "He was in this very place."

"I miss him, too," Aunt Melody said. She looked at her watch. "Our tour doesn't start for thirty minutes. Let's look at the museum."

Displays in glass cases told the story of "the Force," as it's called, from the earliest days. Old movie posters showed handsome stars who'd played Mounties in classic Hollywood epics with titles like *Man from Montreal, Rose Marie,* and *North West Mounted Police*.

I glanced at my aunt. "How many names have the Mounties had, anyway?"

"First, they were the North West Mounted Police. Then 'Royal' was added to the name. Finally, they became the Royal Canadian Mounted Police, or Mounties for short."

I looked at the beautiful eyes and smile of Patricia Dane, who'd starred in *Northwest Rangers*. "She reminds me of Winter Leigh. Speaking of Winter Leigh, apparently she has doubled her reward for the safe return of the Sacred Egyptian Cat." I glanced at my aunt. "I've been thinking about your idea, Aunt Melody— that I find the golden statue. The case certainly needs input from a great detective, don't you think?"

"Indeed, it does. Get on the case, Liz, and you'll be Nancy Drew the Second!" As we left the museum, Aunt Melody said, "Squire has invited us out for dinner tonight. We're going to a steak house."

"But you're a vegetarian."

"Apparently the restaurant also serves delicious fish." She looked at me. "I've been thinking about Billy Bones. Have you read *The Secret of Happiness* yet?"

I shook my head. "So far, we've been too busy. I want to savour the book, so I'm waiting for the right time."

"It's still in your pack?"

"Yup. *The Secret* is with us, even as we speak."

*   *   *

At the parade square, tourists were watching recruits practise marching. As an officer barked commands, they wheeled back and forth under the hot sun while we took pictures.

"Aunt Melody, I just love the little chapel with the red roof. Can we take a look?"

It was cool and quiet inside. The dark wooden walls were lined with brass plaques in memory of former Mounties. We tiptoed forward, staring at two beautiful stained-glass windows behind the altar. Each showed a man in red serge mourning fallen comrades.

"Don't sit in the front pew," Aunt Melody warned. "Your gramps told me it's reserved for the British royal family."

"Wow! Too bad they're not here today—I'd love to see Prince William."

I thought the most interesting part of our tour was a gym where we saw recruits learning judo. An instructor explained how she would use an opponent's weight in self-defence, then demonstrated the skill by easily toppling a large male recruit. "They look so young," Aunt Melody whispered to me. "But soon they'll be out in the real world, protecting us from harm."

"I was *so* happy when those Mounties arrived at the farm," I said.

* * *

That evening, Squire took us to an extremely fancy steak house. The maître d' wore a black tuxedo, everyone spoke in hushed tones, and classical music soothed our ears. I was glad I'd brought a pretty dress on our vacation.

It was a nice evening, and I enjoyed discussing the events at Benbow Farm with Squire. Everything was fine until just after they served dessert. Squire took a big gulp from his glass, then suddenly spat water all over the floor! I was horrified, so was Aunt Melody.

The maitre d' came running. "What's wrong, sir?"

"Look!" Squire pointed a trembling finger at his water glass. "*Look*!"

In the glass was a big black fly.

"Sir," exclaimed the shocked maitre d'. "Sir, I apologize. This is terrible, just terrible."

"I'll sue! Your restaurant will be ruined."

"Please, don't. I'll tell you what, your meal is free."

"For all three of us?"

"Of course."

"Well . . . " Squire thought for a moment, then nodded. "We accept."

"Wonderful! Thank you so much."

The grateful maitre d' escorted us to the door. Outside, Squire rubbed his stomach in satisfaction. "Nothing tastes better than a free meal." Chuckling, he showed us a handful of plastic black flies. "I got these at the joke shop. Handy little things, aren't they?"

Back home, Squire put the car in the garage and locked the door. I looked around at the night—cozy lights glowed in other homes, but I still felt strangely lonely.

Then something moved at an upstairs window. I looked up quickly, but it was only a curtain blowing in the warm wind. "Is that a deck on top of your garage?" I asked Squire.

He nodded. "That's where I work on my tan. The deck connects to the master bedroom."

"Yes—I see the door. It's open."

Startled, Squire looked up. "You're right! But it was locked when we left, I'm sure of it." He hurried up the porch steps to the front door. He inserted his key, the door creaked open, and he looked inside.

"Oh no," he exclaimed. "There's been a break-in!"

* * *

Squire reached for a switch, lighting up the living room. "Look at my writing desk!" He walked quickly over to the corner. The desk drawers were open, and papers littered the floor. "This is terrible," Squire moaned. "I can't believe it!"

He studied the room—it was a mess. "Somebody's been searching. I wonder what for?"

"It wasn't our IMAX tickets," I said. "They're still on your desk." Then I snapped my fingers. "I bet those bikers followed us here."

"But why?" Squire demanded.

"Because maybe I've got what they're looking for." Slipping off my backpack, I took out *The Secret of Happiness*. Closely watched by Aunt Melody and Squire, I opened it—and got a big surprise. The book was a fake, with a hollow in the middle.

In the hollow lay a small, shiny disk.

*   *   *

Grabbing the disk, Squire walked straight to his computer. But it had been vandalized, so he ran to the closet for a laptop.

As the screen glowed to life, Squire turned to me.

"What's the password, Liz? The one Billy Bones gave you, just before he died."

I hesitated. "I'm not sure . . . "

"Hey, come on! This disk could mean serious money. Let's look at it."

"Okay," I agreed, "but I'm not telling you the password, Squire. Please move away from the laptop."

Looking sulky, Squire went to the window. As he stared at the dark night, I entered NOEL. Strange shapes and patterns appeared on the screen. "Aunt Melody and Squire," I said, "come have a look."

They hurried to my side. "Computers are my thing," Squire said, sitting down at the laptop. "This disk is the latest technology. It was programmed by somebody clever, using inscribing software and a miniaturized drive."

We watched anxiously as Squire worked, muttering to himself. "We're almost there," he said at last, then added, "Bingo!"

On the screen, we saw DIEFENBAKER 19_ _. "What does that mean?" Aunt Melody asked.

"It's probably some kind of code," Squire replied.

I looked at him. "John Diefenbaker was the prime minister from Saskatchewan, right?"

Squire nodded. "They called him Dief the Chief. He was one of Canada's great political leaders."

"His nickname was Dief?"

"That's right. What of it?"

"Just before he died, Billy Bones said something about Dief."

Squire stared at me. "Well, what did he say?"

"'Dief died in—.' Those were his last words."

"Excellent!" From an encyclopedia, Squire learned that John G. Diefenbaker had died in 1979. He entered 79 into the code. Instantly, something new appeared on the screen: SUKANEN 19_ _ 50° 31' 14", 105° 63' 21".

"Compass directions," Squire said. "Lines of latitude and longitude. If I'm not mistaken, those coordinates intersect in Saskatchewan." Grabbing an atlas from his reference library, he opened to a map of the province. "Yes! They meet just south of Moose Jaw."

"I wonder what's there?" Aunt Melody said.

"Buried treasure," I exclaimed. "I bet you anything!"

Aunt Melody winked at me. "Is this a Nancy Drew theory?"

Squire peered at me through narrowed eyes. "What kind of treasure?"

"The Sacred Egyptian Cat! The police in L.A. think bikers may have stolen the statue. I bet they brought the golden cat to Canada, and buried it near Moose Jaw."

"Saskatchewan's a long ride from Hollywood. Why would those scoundrels bring it here?"

"I don't know—but it's possible. We should contact the Mounties right away."

Squire looked out the window, thinking. "No," he said at last, "I don't buy your theory, Liz. This disk isn't anything important." He yawned and stretched, then looked at me. "Tell you what. Lend me the disk. I'll travel to where those compass coordinates meet, and see what's there. But I caution you—it's unlikely I'll find anything."

I thought for a moment. "Okay, Squire, you can borrow the disk."

"Excellent!"

"But only if we go with you."

Squire shook his head. "I'm sorry, but that's impossible."

"Then I'd better give the disk to the Mounties."

"No, don't do that!" Squire walked around the room, snapping his fingers. "Okay," he said at last, "you win. You're both invited on the expedition."

"Hooray!" I cried, and danced in a circle. "We're going after treasure!"

Aunt Melody raised her hand. "Just a minute, Liz. I'm not sure about this idea."

"Oh, Aunt Melody, please! This way, I won't get bored. Besides, we left Benbow Farm early. We've got a couple of extra days with nothing planned."

"It could be dangerous, Liz. Bikers broke in here—they might return."

"Bikers?" I shook my head. "I doubt it, Aunt Melody. That was just a weak theory of mine."

Squire nodded. "Local kids are probably the guilty ones," he told my aunt soothingly. "Nothing's been stolen, Melody. Let's not worry about it."

"Shouldn't we call the police?"

Squire thought for a moment, then nodded. "A friend of mine is a senior officer with the RCMP. I'll get her advice, first thing tomorrow morning."

"Well, maybe . . . "

"Oh please, Aunt Melody," I begged.

"Okay, but only for a couple of days." She turned to Squire. "Who's paying for this expedition? I'm a student, so I can't afford it."

"No problem. I'll make all the arrangements."

"How will we travel? By Greyhound?"

"I've got the perfect idea," Squire replied. "A man named Arrow lives over on Victoria Avenue. He's converted a school bus into a travelling motor home. You hire Arrow as the driver, and he'll take you anywhere. His girlfriend, Teresa, comes along as cook. Last year, I went north with them on a fishing holiday. I drool at the memory of Teresa's fabulous bannock. Later tonight, I'll phone the Great Plains Bar on North Railway. That's where Teresa works—she makes all the arrangements."

"What's bannock?" I asked.

"It's a kind of bread. It's delicious with jam, just delicious." Squire rubbed his stomach. "I absolutely love Teresa's bannock."

"What will you tell them about the disk?" Aunt Melody asked.

"As little as possible—mum's the word. I'll tell them we want to take a fishing trip."

"This will be fun!" I looked at Squire. "May I please have the disk?"

He seemed startled. "Um . . . well . . . I'm not sure . . . "

Aunt Melody looked at him. "Billy Bones gave Liz the book, Squire. So the disk is hers."

"I guess you're right. But take good care of it, Liz. Okay?"

"It'll be in my backpack." I yawned. "Suddenly, I feel very sleepy. Good night, folks."

Pack in hand, I slowly climbed to the second floor. All the excitement had worn me out. Upstairs, I tried the light switch, but it didn't work. The hallway was completely dark.

I heard Aunt Melody and Squire talking in the living room. Squinting, I felt my way forward into the blackness. I remembered that my door was the second on the left; when I got there, I could flick on the bedroom light.

But when I reached for the switch, my fingers touched the warmth of someone's face.

* * *

I yelled in horror.

A shape moved in the darkness as a hand seized my pack. But I wouldn't let go, and desperately fought the intruder for control.

Feet pounded up the stairs. "We're coming, Liz!" Squire yelled.

"Hurry!"

The person let go of my pack. I saw the dark shape of the intruder escape through Squire's bedroom to the deck, climb over the railing, and disappear. As Squire and Aunt Melody ran into the room, I rushed out onto the deck to see a black shape below, escaping into the night.

I wanted to give chase, but Squire held me back. "We'll let the police deal with this. I'll phone them immediately. You two, wait downstairs."

As he picked up the bedroom phone, we left the room. Aunt Melody was very upset and wanted to leave immediately for Winnipeg, but I calmed her down. Things were getting interesting, and I didn't intend to go home!

"Let's go outside," I suggested to Aunt Melody, "and watch for the police to arrive. I'm not sleepy anymore."

Moonlight bathed the trees and lawn of Squire's front yard. Wandering across the grass, we stopped beside a wooden fence. The neighbour's yard contained many dark bushes and trees; I made out the dim shape of a hammock strung between two sturdy trunks.

"Perhaps we'd better go home," Aunt Melody said. "That attack's got me very concerned, Liz."

"The break-in was *nothing*, Aunt Melody. Just local kids, or something like that. Besides, it was your suggestion that I get started as a detective."

"But I was only kidding, Liz!"

"What if Tom finds a case before I do? This is important, Aunt Melody."

Squire came outside. "I spoke to the police. They don't want us to worry. An officer will be here in the morning."

"Not before?" Aunt Melody asked.

"They're busy," Squire replied. "Besides, nothing's been stolen."

"But Liz was attacked!"

"That's why they are sending an officer," Squire said. "But not until morning. At the moment all their people are investigating more serious crimes."

"Do the police think the intruder was after the computer disk?" Aunt Melody asked.

"They didn't say."

We stood together for a while, discussing the events of the evening. Then I heard a noise from the other side of the fence. A man got out of the hammock—he was wearing dark clothing, so I hadn't noticed him before.

"Smollett," Squire exclaimed. "You were snooping on our conversation!"

"I was lying in my hammock, neighbour. You have a loud voice, so I couldn't help hearing."

Smollett looked about Squire's age, but was much smaller. He was dressed in jeans and a T-shirt—both black—and was wearing a dark baseball cap without a logo. Smollett reminded me of a coiled snake, ready to snap with venomous fangs. I felt wary of him from the moment we met.

"So," he said to Squire, "you've found a disk, and you're planning a treasure expedition. Very interesting."

"This is none of your business," Squire protested.

"I smell money in the air. You owe me plenty, mister."

"When I hit the jackpot, you'll be the first to know."

"I'd better not be the last." Smollett raised his baseball cap to us; his hair was thick and wiry. "Good night, ladies." He looked at Squire with a smirk. "Good night, neighbour. I hope you do find buried treasure, because most of it will belong to me."

Smollett went into his house and closed the door. "That guy really bugs me," Squire said. "I've known him for years. He's a pest."

Aunt Melody looked at him. "Squire, are you okay for money? This expedition could get expensive."

"It's no problem, Melody, but thanks for asking."

* * *

After all the excitement, falling asleep took a long time. In the morning, enjoying a late breakfast, I was surprised to learn that the police hadn't yet arrived.

"I'll phone them again," Squire said, consulting his watch. "But first I'll drive you to the IMAX theatre. You've got reserved seats for today's first show, don't forget."

He dropped us outside the theatre. "After the show," he said, "enjoy a walk in the park. It's beautiful."

The theatre was located in Wascana Park, a cool paradise on a hot day. The trees were radiant with their new leaves, and luxurious green grass covered undulating slopes beside the blue, blue waters of a large lake. People were out in sailboats, and I saw a war canoe filled with happy kids.

The theatre overlooked the water. It was a huge building, big enough to contain a screen five storeys high. Several yellow school buses were parked nearby. "I feel deliciously guilty missing school," I said to Aunt Melody with a happy sigh.

We purchased popcorn and raspberry lemonade, then climbed a lot of stairs. I was amazed by the screen's size; facing it were many rows of seats, rising steeply.

Most were occupied by school kids. As we found our seats, I listened to them laughing and talking together. Then a teacher in a green dress startled everyone with a piercing whistle. "You students from Sunningdale School—do not put your feet on the chairs in front. And remember, your food is to be eaten, not thrown around."

The lights went down. The kids burst into cheers and whistles, then suddenly fell silent as a huge image filled the screen. It was a black sky, glowing with stars. Then we experienced a tumbling ride down a strange tunnel before confronting the roaring lava flames of an exploding volcano.

Aunt Melody and I gazed in astonishment at enormous images of red-hot ash, and giant boulders flying through the air. Not a single kid in the audience spoke as we watched Nature unleash its furies.

To tell the truth, the show was so exciting, I completely forgot about Billy Bones and the disk with its secret code. But they popped back in my mind the moment the movie ended. Descending the stairs to the lobby, I thought about our upcoming trip. "Just think, Aunt Melody, we may find the golden statue!"

She frowned. "I'm still not sure we should be . . . "

"Did you speak to Mom and Dad?"

Aunt Melody shook her head. "They've been delayed at that lawyers' convention. But I said hello to Tom. He says lucky you, finding an adventure."

"He's right!"

In the washroom, Aunt Melody applied lipstick while I chattered away about volcanoes and earthquakes. Then a cubicle door opened, and a woman stepped out. She was young, but wore a drab, old-fashioned dress. Her long black hair hung in tangles.

"Please," she begged. "You've got to help me!"

5

Aunt Melody stared at her. "What's wrong?"

"A man has threatened me. I must get to a taxi, but I'm afraid."

Aunt Melody turned to me. "Liz, go see if there's a cab available."

It was hot outside. I ran to a taxi, asked the driver to wait, then watched Aunt Melody bring the young woman from the theatre—she looked very frightened.

Reaching the cab, the woman hesitated. "I'm broke," she told Aunt Melody. "I can't afford a taxi."

"I'll pay for it," my aunt offered.

"No!" The woman backed away, shaking her head. "I could never do that." Her gaze swept the parking lot, and she swallowed nervously. "I'll be okay. I'll walk to the bus. I can afford the bus."

"We'll go with you."

The young woman's green eyes brightened. "That would be so kind! I'll catch a bus on Albert Street—it's through the park." As we started walking, she lit a cigarette. "My name is Candy."

Except for her messy black hair, Candy was quite pretty. Her ears had been pierced multiple times, but her only jewellery was a ruby-coloured glass ring. As we followed the path along the water, Candy kept looking over her shoulder.

"What's the problem?" Aunt Melody asked. "What happened, Candy?"

"My old man skipped town, owing money all over." Candy was close to tears. "Now people are after me, trying to get it back. Scary guys have been knocking on my door."

"What happened at the IMAX?"

"Some guy threatened me. But I'm broke," she wailed unhappily. "I can't give them the money!" With trembling hands, Candy lit a cigarette. "I've got to get away from Regina. I wanna go home."

"Where are you from?" I asked.

"Moose Jaw. It's west of Regina, on the cross-Canada highway." Candy turned to my aunt. "If I could get home to Moose Jaw, I'd be safe."

Aunt Melody paused, thinking. "I've got an idea." When we reached Albert Street, she found a pay phone. "I'm calling Squire," she told me. "Maybe he can help."

Candy lit another cigarette. Moving upwind, I watched the park for signs of trouble. Then Aunt

Melody approached with a big smile on her face. "Guess what, Candy! We're giving you a lift to Moose Jaw. My cousin has arranged to hire a bus, and there's room for you."

Candy's green eyes lit up with happiness. "Bless you," she said, grabbing Aunt Melody's hand, and pumping it up and down. "Bless you!"

*   *   *

The *Mañana Banana* arrived early the next morning.

My bedroom at Squire's house overlooked the street. I was getting ready for the trip when I heard a *quack!* from outside. I looked for a passing duck—but then realized that I'd heard the unusual horn of a yellow school bus parked out front.

"They're here," I called, rushing outside. The words *Mañana Banana* decorated the hood of the bus; inside, I saw peace symbols above the windows and hand-painted flowers. A row of tiny multicoloured elephants stretched along the dashboard.

Aunt Melody examined the tires. "The tread looks fine. I guess we'll be safe."

Squire waved at the man behind the wheel. "Good morning, Arrow!"

He was about thirty-five and wore boots, faded jeans, and a denim jacket over a white T-shirt. Was he ever handsome! His dark brown eyes crinkled when he smiled at me, and he had the most amazing cheekbones—they'd take top prize in any search for the perfect face.

After the introductions, Squire handed a cheque to

Arrow. I thought Squire looked a bit worried. "Here's full payment for the first week."

Nodding his thanks, Arrow casually shoved the cheque into the hip pocket of his jeans. Then I saw Candy walking towards us with a bright red backpack. She looked better today, more self-confident. She'd even tried to do something with her black hair, but without much success. I itched to give her some styling tips.

Candy thanked Squire politely for the lift to Moose Jaw. Then she turned to Arrow. "Hi there," she said, fluttering the lashes of her big green eyes. "I'm Candy. Is this your bus? It's cool."

"Thanks!" Arrow smiled proudly. Then he looked at Squire. "I've got bad news—we don't have a cook."

Squire's mouth fell open. "*What*?"

"Teresa walked out on me." Arrow was angry. "I put so much into that relationship and now she dumps me."

"What terrible news!" Squire marched up and down the sidewalk, greatly agitated. "Teresa's the best cook alive! Her bannock, man! I was really looking forward to it."

Arrow slapped the front of the bus. "Teresa and I fixed this up together," he said bitterly. "It was our business, our future. We had all kinds of dreams." Again, his hand rang against the yellow metal. "I can't believe she's done this to me."

"You poor thing," Candy said. "I'm so sorry. Perhaps . . ."

"Be quiet, woman," Squire interrupted her. "What about our expedition, Arrow? Is it cancelled?"

"Not a chance," he replied. "I survive my disappointments. But I *really* believed in Teresa."

Squire turned to Aunt Melody. "Why don't you volunteer to cook?"

"Why don't *you*?"

Squire shrugged his big shoulders. "Cooking is a girl thing."

"I very much disagree."

It was a tense moment, but luckily Candy saved the day. "I wouldn't mind cooking until we reach Moose Jaw," she said timidly. "People like my meals."

"Done," exclaimed Squire, beaming with pleasure. "I'm delighted we've got a cook. The trip is on—let's load the luggage, everyone!"

I was first in the bus with my stuff, and took the opportunity to look around. A picture over the driver's seat showed the earth from space, and a slogan reminded us to respect our planet. I noticed a stove and a small refrigerator, tables and bus seats bolted to the floor, and a laundry hamper beside a door marked WC.

Arrow was at a table, preparing a logbook for the trip.

"What does WC mean?" I asked.

"*Water closet*. The toilet's behind that door."

"How do the stove and refrigerator work?"

"Propane."

"This is an awesome bus. How do you pronounce that word in its name?"

"Man-yana. It means *tomorrow* in Spanish."

"Where'd you get the *Mañana Banana*?"

"A retired hippie sold it to me and Teresa." Arrow shook his head. "Man, that girl's hurt me."

"What happened? Why did she leave?"

Arrow shrugged. "Who knows? Teresa works nights

at a bar, singing. She usually gets home about three a.m. This morning she never showed up."

"Maybe she was kidnapped. Did you phone the police?"

"Not a chance. I've got a prison record, from when I was a teenager stealing cars. The cops would blame me for her disappearance. They'd probably make me cancel this trip, and I really need the money."

"You think Teresa ran away?"

"Yeah, maybe. We've been fighting lately. Teresa wants to be a country-and-western star, but I want us to settle down together."

"Operating the *Mañana Banana*?"

Arrow shook his head. "I want to get a small farm, and raise organic vegetables to sell. Maybe have some kids. Teresa's got a daughter—she's really nice, but I want a bunch of children around. You kids have so much energy for life."

"So you figure Teresa ran away to become a singer?"

"Maybe, or else she's gone back to the streets. I don't know what to think!"

I looked at Arrow's dark eyes. They were full of pain.

"Back to the streets? What do you mean?"

Arrow produced a crumpled piece of paper. Crude letters printed with lipstick said *Don't look for me. I really mean this. Please respect my wishes*. The note was signed with the letter *T*.

"She wears that colour lipstick?" I asked.

"Sure. Hers is red, just like on this note."

"But there are many shades of red. What was her

favourite? Rose Petal? Beverley Hills Blush?"

Arrow shook his head. "I don't know. But I'm respecting Teresa's wishes. I'm not looking for her."

I couldn't think of any more questions—so much for being Nancy Drew! As I sat down, feeling rueful, Squire and Aunt Melody climbed on board with their luggage.

"By the way," she said to Squire, "what happened about your friend at the RCMP? Do the Mounties want to see the disk?"

Turning his face, Squire coughed. Then he took out a handkerchief and carefully wiped his mouth. He folded the handkerchief, returned it to his pocket, and finally looked at Aunt Melody again. "The Mounties have asked me to investigate any leads provided by the disk. After we've been to Moose Jaw, I'll report to them. Meanwhile, they'll continue investigating the tragic events at Benbow Farm."

"What about the city police? They're supposed to investigate last night's intruder."

"We've no time for that," Squire replied impatiently. "Liz wasn't harmed. I'll call the cops again, when we get home. Meanwhile, we're in a big hurry."

Arrow glanced at him. "What's the rush? The fish will be biting, whenever we get there."

"You're right." Squire winked at my aunt, then turned to Arrow with an innocent face. "Of course, they will. But my relatives have only a few days for this fishing trip, and we're anxious to get going."

"Okay," Arrow said. "Let's take off, then."

A door slammed at a nearby house. Smollett came down the street towards us, carrying a nylon haversack.

It matched his all-black look: cap, T-shirt, jeans.

His eyes flicked over us. "I'm going with you," he announced. "If you find anything, I want my share. Besides, Squire, you're probably operating this expedition on a wing and a prayer. If you run out of money, I've got deep pockets."

Squire's face brightened. "Then let's get on the road."

Arrow waved at Candy, who sat with a cigarette in the shade of a tree. "We're leaving!"

As she stood up, Smollett's eyes widened. "That gorgeous female is part of the trip? Now I'm *really* glad I joined you." Walking over to Candy, Smollett presented his business card. She accepted it, but didn't seem impressed.

* * *

As we drove through Regina, I sat near Arrow, watching him drive the bus (and admiring his face). It was an overcast, muggy day. Dust and dried blossoms were being blown through the streets, and fat raindrops splattered against the windshield.

"May I ask a favour, Arrow? On the map, I see a town called Avonlea. Would it be okay to visit there, on our way to Moose Jaw?"

"That's a major detour, Liz. Why's Avonlea so important?"

"My favourite author is Lucy Maud Montgomery— she's famous for books about Avonlea. It's supposed to be in P.E.I., but she once lived in Saskatchewan. Maybe she visited this town for inspiration! I'm just dying to find out."

Arrow glanced up at the mirror, where Squire's glum face was reflected. "Can we spend a few dollars on extra gas, boss?"

"Not a chance—I'm anxious to reach Moose Jaw."

Aunt Melody looked at Squire. "You owe me money for the taxi fare. Until you repay me, I'm part owner of this expedition."

"Oh, for pity's sake," Squire grumbled, looking sulky.

"As part owner," Aunt Melody continued, "I've decided we're going to visit Avonlea."

"Great," I exclaimed.

Arrow grinned at me, and Smollett's face cracked in a smile. "Well, Squire, you've met your match. It's about time a woman stood up to your bullying ways."

"Drop on your head," Squire muttered.

Before long, we were south of Regina on Highway 6. We passed a couple of radio transmission towers and a drive-in movie theatre with a sign that read CLOSED DUE TO FLOODING. There was water everywhere, making the big screen look forlorn.

Aunt Melody dug around in her pack for a cassette. "I see you've got a tape deck," she said to Arrow. "Do you mind playing some of my favourites?"

"Sure," Arrow replied. "That would cheer me up."

I don't know if the others were expecting opera, but that's what we got. Actually it's not bad stuff, once you get adjusted. It felt nice listening to the luxurious voices of the singers while travelling past green, green fields that stretched to the horizon under stormy skies.

Aunt Melody kept getting Arrow to stop the bus.

She'd jump off, take a picture of something, then leap back on board. Her camera produced instant pictures, so we got to enjoy her artistry. My personal favourite was a red barn framed between the black sky and an emerald field, but Arrow voted for a distant grain elevator rising above the horizon.

"I'm dying for a cigarette," Candy said.

"No smoking on the bus!" Squire barked.

"Give the lady a break," Smollett sneered at Squire. "She needs her cigarette."

Arrow pointed at a highway sign. "Let's stop at that historic site."

The moment the bus stopped, Candy jumped off. As she lit up, the rest of us left the bus to stretch our legs. I watched Aunt Melody photograph the sign that described the site. "According to this sign," she said, "a famous trail once passed this way. It was used by Native peoples, traders, missionaries, and the first Mounties. The famous American rebel Chief Sitting Bull passed by here with his people, when they sought sanctuary north of the border."

Back on the *Mañana Banana*, Candy pulled a tabloid newspaper out of her backpack. "Anything new on the golden statue?" I asked.

"Actually," she replied, "this is an old issue. There's a great picture of the cat—that's why I kept it." Candy showed me the statue, which looked magnificent in the photo. "Isn't it wonderful, Liz? Do you know, the golden statue is a replica of the Sacred Bast Cat. Bast was a goddess, revered by the ancient Egyptians."

I stared at the picture. "That statue must be *fabulous* to actually see."

Candy nodded. "You're right."

Smollett had been listening to our conversation. Now he turned to Squire. There was a smile on Smollett's bony face. "I've just figured something out."

Squire ignored him.

"Yes," Smollett said, "it all adds up! I know exactly what this expedition is searching for."

Arrow looked at Smollett in the rearview mirror. "We're searching for fish."

Squire quickly nodded his agreement. "Yes—fish. That's what we're after."

"Fishing—of course." Smollett glanced slyly around at our faces. "The question is, fishing for what?"

* * *

After a long drive, we approached Avonlea. It was a small community, nestled at the foot of low hills. A beautiful sign welcomed us, so we stopped for pictures. The sign was shaped like a huge arrowhead; a plaque explained that the sign honoured the Native peoples of this region.

"I'm disappointed there's no reference to Lucy Maud Montgomery," I said.

"Let's ask downtown," Arrow suggested. "Climb on board, everybody."

Avonlea was a pretty town with leafy, tree-lined streets. The main street was very wide, with lots of stores and banks; no building was more than a storey high. At the foot of Main Street, a classic train station graced Railway Avenue. Kids rode past on bikes, and I saw a yellow bus with the words PRAIRIE VIEW SCHOOL DISTRICT. A Canadian flag snapped in the wind over the post office; nearby was a small library. "Let's try there," I suggested.

Arrow parked outside a bank. "I'm going to cash Squire's cheque," he said, as we climbed off the bus. "There's stuff I need to buy, real bad."

Squire swallowed hard. His skin turned pale, darkening the shadows under his eyes. He watched Arrow disappear inside the bank, then said, "I'm going for a coffee."

"I'll join you," Smollett declared. "But first, I'm calling my office for messages."

"Come with us, Candy," Squire said.

"Perfect," I whispered to my aunt. "We can investigate at the library, just the two of us." As we walked to the library, I looked at my aunt. "I think Smollett has figured out my theory—that we're going to find the golden statue."

Aunt Melody seemed doubtful. "Probably the sacred cat is somewhere in California. I think Winter Leigh will increase the reward. Then the thief will turn it in."

I didn't agree, but said nothing more. The library's lobby announced forthcoming community events, and invited kids to join a summer reading program. A friendly woman welcomed us, and nodded when I asked about Lucy Maud Montgomery. "A lot of Maud's fans visit here. We believe that her relatives were early pioneers who named Avonlea in her honour. But nobody's certain."

I found a couple of *Anne* books on the shelf, and touched them for luck. Then, back outside, we came upon a nasty scene.

DONTIANEN

6

Arrow had Squire pinned against the side of the bus. His fist was raised—Squire looked terrified.

Aunt Melody cried, "*Stop!*"

Arrow hesitated, giving Squire the chance to squirm away. "You crazy man," Squire yelled, taking shelter behind Smollett. "I'll tell my lawyer about you."

"Your cheque bounced! It's useless! We'll have to cancel the expedition." Turning to the bus, Arrow slammed his hand against the hot metal. "More bad luck! I'm jinxed!"

I turned unhappily to my aunt. "Our trip is ruined, Aunt Melody."

Candy burst into tears. "I'll never get home to

Moose Jaw," she wailed. With trembling hands, she quickly lit a cigarette. "What'll I do? What'll I do?"

I felt just as emotional as Candy. Our great adventure had crashed in flames. Glumly, I stared at the sidewalk, feeling cheated.

Then Smollett saved the day. "I'll invest some money," he said, glancing at Candy as she smiled in relief. "I could use some adventure in my life."

Smollett discussed the financial terms with Arrow, then went into the bank and soon returned, clutching a wad of cash. "Let's hit the road," he told Arrow, shoving the money into his hand.

Quickly, Arrow counted the bills. "Let's get moving," Squire said, consulting his watch. "We're running late."

"I suggest making camp overnight in a field," Arrow said. "A friend of mine has a farm nearby."

"But . . . " Squire spluttered. "But . . . we're in a hurry! Let's drive all night."

Aunt Melody shook her head. "Not a chance—that's dangerous. Arrow, please head for that farm."

Squire muttered angrily, but said nothing more. Smollett chuckled. "I'm enjoying this trip already." He winked at Candy. "Are you?"

"So far," she replied, looking at Arrow.

*   *   *

Before long, the *Mañana Banana* was puttering along Route 339. There wasn't much traffic; little birds waited on the road as we approached, then flew off at the last possible second. The golden light of a perfect sunset reflected off rows of metal storage sheds, and a wind played among the trees that sheltered farmhouses.

"Why take all those pictures?" Smollett asked Aunt Melody, as her shutter clicked again.

"There's so much beauty around us. I want to preserve it somehow."

"I like the thought," Smollett said. "I should take up photography as a hobby. Life can get boring, even with lots of money."

The bus turned onto a dirt road. Just above the horizon, a low bank of clouds reflected the sunset's final colours. This area seemed really empty; when we finally passed a car, the driver waved a greeting. The prairie turned into murky shadows, and I wondered if we'd ever make camp.

At last, the bus stopped. Dust swirled around the headlights as I stared into the darkness. Nothing could be seen. The others seemed groggy as they followed Arrow off the bus. The air was cold. I could hear the sounds of insects in the night.

"They're probably discussing us," I said. "We're alien invaders of their territory."

Before long, we were seated around a campfire, watching Candy pour batter into a hot frying pan. "Whatcha making?" I asked.

"Cornmeal cakes." Candy glanced at me with her green eyes. "I hope you'll like them."

"My mouth is watering." I looked at the parrot pin on her sweater; silver words said *Pieces of Eight*. "Did your boyfriend give you that?"

Candy shook her head. "I don't have one."

I glanced at her tangled black hair. "I bet my aunt

could help with your hair. She's done mine a lot."

"No," Candy exclaimed. "Not a chance."

"Okay, no problem," I said, surprised at her reaction.

Arrow poured coffee from a blackened pot. Then he smiled at Smollett. "It's really great that you saved the expedition, sir. I'd like to say thanks."

"Think nothing of it, Arrow. I've got plenty of money."

Candy announced the meal was ready. She was a great cook. Her cornmeal cakes had everyone begging for more. Then she passed around a bag of nice, soft marshmallows. Toasting a white blob of sugar on a stick, I looked at the dark night just as a shooting star burned across the sky. "Another soul gone to heaven," I said. The distant whistle of a train added a touch of romance to the scene. The fresh air was clean and delicious—until Candy lit a cigarette.

I turned to Arrow. "Is it fun—having your own business?"

"It's good and bad. I've always wanted to farm, maybe grow organic vegetables, but running the *Banana* is okay for now."

"How'd you meet Teresa?"

"I had a job with the government in Regina. I'd go into the streets of the city, helping hard-luck people. I was in a bar one night when a chick stood up in the audience and volunteered to sing. That was Teresa. What a voice!"

Arrow sighed, staring into the flames. Their colours danced across his handsome face. "We moved in together. Soon after, the government cut back and I lost my job."

"That's tragic," Candy said.

"I'm not a quitter, Candy. I decided to start a company. I'm a Cree and Teresa is Métis, from a place called Willow Bunch, so we decided to establish a tourist business that would make use of our knowledge of Native regions of Saskatchewan. It was going fine—until she disappeared on me."

"What happened?" Candy asked.

"To make extra money, Teresa sang every night in a bar. Last night she didn't come home. I went looking for her. The bartender said a gang of bikers had been drinking in the bar. They left before Teresa finished her gig, but maybe she met them later."

"Were the bikers from California?" I asked.

"The bartender didn't say." Arrow sighed. "Teresa's fascinated by motorcycles and all that stuff. The bartender said she was laughing and talking with the bikers all evening. I bet she ran away with them."

"Or maybe they kidnapped her," I suggested.

Candy nodded her agreement. "Did you call the cops?" she asked Arrow.

"Nope. They wouldn't believe me. Anyway, who cares? I'm a loser at love. Maybe Teresa ran away with those bikers, maybe she's chasing her dream to be a singer. Either way, we're finished. It's sad, but true."

* * *

We were on the road early the next morning. I stared out the window while my aunt studied for her exams. "You know what, Aunt Melody?" I whispered. "Today, we arrive at the coordinates of latitude and longitude. I bet we'll find the golden cat."

"Uh huh," she mumbled vaguely, eyes focused on her notes.

Giving up on getting her attention, I grabbed a juice from the refrigerator and went to sit near Arrow as the *Mañana Banana* turned onto the Trans-Canada Highway.

Despite the early hour, there was a lot of traffic on the nation's main drag. Above the busy road the sky was pink, awaiting the sun; when the fireball slowly rose above the horizon, its light was reflected from the chrome bumpers of big transports rushing past. Farmhouses and barns turned golden as morning arrived in all its radiance.

Arrow smiled at me from the wheel. "Beautiful scene, huh? See the highrise towers ahead? That's downtown Moose Jaw."

Squire looked at Arrow. "According to my calculations, our destination is about 13 clicks south of Moose Jaw on Highway 2."

"Where did the name Moose Jaw come from?" I asked Arrow.

Smollett looked up from a magazine. "I know that one. History is a hobby of mine. You see—"

Squire noisily cleared his throat, interrupting Smollett. "Pioneers once used the jaw of a moose to make emergency repairs to a Red River cart," he proclaimed. "That's how the city got its name."

"You are wrong," Smollett said firmly. "The name comes from the Cree word *moosegaw*, meaning *warm breezes*. Isn't that correct, Arrow?"

"Yup."

"Hmmmph," Squire muttered, but he didn't argue the point.

Highway 2 wasn't as busy as the Trans-Canada. It ran in a straight line between fields green with new crops, under skies where birds soared on the winds of an approaching storm. A gas station displayed a sign that read HONK IF YOU FEEL GOOD, but Arrow didn't touch the horn. There was tension in the air, especially between Squire and Smollett.

"I'll check our position," Squire said. He opened a leather carrying case and removed the laptop. "Would you enter the password, please," he said, passing it to me.

I entered NOEL, then went to stand beside Squire. As he worked, Smollett watched from a chair. "You're quite the hacker, Squire. That's the only reason I'm here. One day your genius with computers will lead you to big money. When that happens, I'll be at your side. My hand will be out, waiting for a refund on all those loans. Plus substantial interest."

"Yeah, yeah," Squire muttered, peering at the laptop screen.

"This software is called SaskMap," he explained to me. "Zoom in on any spot in the province, and SaskMap shows every road, even dirt trails."

"What's the beeping sound?"

"SaskMap is connected to a Global Positioning System satellite. It can pinpoint our location to within a few metres. I've entered the coordinates of latitude and longitude. As we approach the precise place where they meet, the beeping will get louder."

Down the highway, I spotted a collection of small wooden buildings. "It's some kind of old-fashioned western town," I said to Aunt Melody. "Look—there's a railway station, and a church, and pioneer houses. I'd love to explore this place!"

"According to SaskMap," Squire said, "we stop here."

Turning onto a side road, we bumped past a gas station with 1920 over the door, a barber shop, and a newspaper office. The place looked like a movie set—but one thing didn't fit. The scene was dominated by a large wooden boat that rose above the buildings; painted blue, red, and white, it had square windows and a stovepipe sticking out the top. Supported by poles, the boat stood high and dry without any water in sight. "What in the world is that?" I asked. "Is it Noah's ark or something?"

"You're looking at the famous *Dontianen*," Smollett said. "A pioneer built that ship. He was from Finland, and wanted to sail home."

Squire snorted. "What a fool! We're thousands of miles from the ocean. How did he plan to reach it?"

"He figured out a route that connected along different rivers all the way to Hudson Bay. He wanted a vessel big enough to float across the Atlantic to Finland, but died before he completed work on his boat. He never got home."

"That's sad," Aunt Melody said.

Stepping off the bus, we were greeted by a man selling tickets. "Welcome to our pioneer museum," he said. "It's named for Tom Sukanen, who built the *Dontianen*."

Leaning close to Aunt Melody, I whispered, "The code on the disk included the name Sukanen!"

The ticket seller showed us a display of classic cars in mint condition, then invited us to explore the town. "Each building was moved here from its original location. The United Church was built in Tilney in 1907, and the blacksmith's shop opened in Eyebrow in 1936. You'll see the smithy's original equipment inside."

"Eyebrow?" I said. "Is that a real place?"

He nodded. "Saskatchewan's got some unusual names, like Plenty and Horizon." He looked at a crow cawing in a nearby tree, then turned to me. "Quick—help me spot a second crow. Otherwise, there'll be bad luck for all of us."

"There's another one," I said, pointing.

"Good work!" He shook hands with each of us. "Well, enjoy yourselves."

"One question," Squire said. "What year did Tom Sukanen die?"

"Look on his gravestone—he's buried beside the boat."

As we hurried towards the *Dontianen,* I said to Aunt Melody, "Maybe the Sacred Egyptian Cat's hidden on board!"

"Don't get too excited, Liz. Just enjoy the trip—I don't think we'll be finding any golden statues."

"I'm not so sure, Aunt Melody."

The boat rose high above. A sign dedicated the site TO ALL EARLY PIONEERS TO WHOM WE OWE SO MUCH. "It's true," Aunt Melody said. "They worked so hard."

A tiny chapel stood near the boat. Beside it was a grave with a cross and a bronze plaque that said *Tom Sukanen, Died April 23, 1943, Age 55, SHIPBUILDER.*

"This is it!" cried Squire. He called up SUKANEN 19_ _ on the laptop screen, then entered 43. The screen blinked and a new code appeared: THOMPSON NWMP 19_ _ 49° 33' 17", 106° 29' 42".

"Eureka!" Squire jumped up and down. "The code works! We'll find the treasure and be rich!" He turned to Arrow. "We must leave immediately for the next location."

"Okay, but what's going on? Is this some kind of treasure hunt?"

"Maybe, maybe! But don't quote me, my good friend."

Squire was so excited, I thought he'd explode. Smollett watched him from under those shaggy eyebrows, saying nothing. On his sour mouth was a tiny smile.

I looked at Candy, who'd wandered away to smoke a cigarette. "She seems bored by everything."

"Except for cooking," Aunt Melody said with a smile. "Candy's meals are truly marvellous."

"I think she's trying to impress Arrow."

"I can't say I blame her. Arrow's a very nice man."

Squire was impatient to leave, but Aunt Melody wanted to explore the pioneer museum. "Give us an hour. Come on, Liz, we'll visit the *Dontianen* first."

Inside the ship, hand-lettered displays told the story of Tom Sukanen. A framed hospital card revealed that he'd been born in 1881, and we saw his sad eyes in a self-portrait taken with a camera he'd made himself. Tom Sukanen was quite the inventor—we also learned he'd turned a small shed and a motor into the world's first snowmobile!

I searched around for the golden cat, but of course

found nothing. "I wish there was a guide," I said, "so we could ask questions."

"It's kind of a do-it-yourself museum, I guess. This sign says it's operated entirely by volunteers."

I looked out a window at the grave of Tom Sukanen. Squire and Smollett were beside it, arguing angrily. "I wonder what that's all about?"

"They certainly don't get along."

"You know the picture you took of Billy Bones? Let's see if that ticket seller remembers him."

Sure enough, the man recognized Billy Bones. "He had a big motorcycle, I remember. Didn't stay long."

"Just long enough to make a code," I said to Aunt Melody as we explored the general store, but she didn't respond. We wandered through the muggy heat to the railway station, which faced a short length of track. On the platform, leather suitcases and big trunks were lined up, waiting for trains that would never arrive.

Upstairs, we saw the living quarters for the station agent and his family. "It feels strange being here," I said, looking at an 1888 christening gown on display beside a wedding dress worn by Mrs. Daisy Fowler in 1912. "There's all this stuff, but no people. It's kind of like a ghost town."

The streets were deserted except for gophers that ran squeaking among their burrows. I saw Arrow going into the fire hall; the others waited for us at the parking lot. Then a yellow bus with WILLOW BUNCH SCHOOL printed on the side pulled off Highway 2 and stopped at the ticket entrance. A group of kids piled off, followed by their teachers.

"Willow Bunch," I said. "Arrow's missing girlfriend is from there."

"What a memory you've got, Liz." Aunt Melody gave me a smile. "I must admit you've got the makings of a good detective." She studied her map of the village. "Let's check out the homesteader's shack."

The place was tiny. A sign informed us that for fifty years it had been home to a pioneer named Will Grimshaw. We saw a cloth cap hanging from the metal frame of his tiny bed. Beside it was a pipe and an ancient checkerboard; on the wooden wall were black-and-white photographs and tinted postcards.

"This photo shows him playing cricket," Aunt Melody said. "He came from Colwyn Bay, England."

"Here's a little girl in a white dress," I said. "His daughter, maybe."

Raindrops splattered against the only window. Aunt Melody looked out at the stormy sky. "How many times did Will Grimshaw watch rain and snow and hail, lonely for his family in England? If only these walls could talk!"

Back outside, we hurried through the rain towards the *Mañana Banana*. The kids from Willow Bunch were sheltering in doorways, waiting out the storm. Big raindrops splattered against my face. "These glasses of mine slip down my nose in the rain," I complained. "Sometimes they fall off. I think I'll get contact lenses."

Suddenly, I stopped. "Aunt Melody, we didn't see the Spicer school! Come on, we've *got* to."

She looked at her watch. "I'd better tell Squire what's happening. I'll meet you inside the school."

"We're not the only ones late." I pointed at Arrow, who was taking shelter beside the 1909 farmhouse.

Aunt Melody hurried off. "See you in a minute," she called.

It felt strange, entering the school alone—it was almost as if I could hear the voices of its long-ago students. They had sat in these same wooden desks, looking at the same maps above the chalkboard. Britain's Union Jack flag hung near the wood stove, a reminder of the country that once ruled Canada.

In a corner was a large apple barrel. I looked inside; it was empty. As I brushed my hair out of my face, my glasses suddenly slipped—I grabbed but missed, and they dropped into the murky depths. Climbing inside, I knelt down to search for my glasses in the gloom. Just as I found them, I heard the front door bang. Expecting to see Aunt Melody, I peeked through a knothole in the side of the barrel—and, instead, saw Arrow.

* * *

He shook rain from his hair. For some reason, I stayed low, hidden inside the barrel. Then I heard the door again. This time, it was a blue-eyed girl with long black hair. She looked about twelve—my age—and wore jeans and a Willow Bunch Giants team jacket. Her brown skin was wet with rain.

"Hi there," Arrow said. "I saw the Willow Bunch school bus, and figured you'd be on it."

"Why'd you sneak in here, Arrow? Trying to avoid me?"

"Of course not, Marie. I wanted to see this school-house, that's all."

Rushing to Arrow, the girl cried, "Where's my mom? What's happened to her?"

"Hey," Arrow said, raising his hands defensively. "Don't lose your cool. Teresa walked out on me. I'm the one with the grievance."

"You're lying!"

Marie tried to hit Arrow, but he easily deflected her fist. Slumping into a desk, she began to sob. Arrow sat at another desk, and leaned towards her. "She'll get in touch with you, Marie," he said gently. "Teresa's probably heading for the coast."

Still weeping into her hands, Marie shook her head. "You remember when Granny gave Mom that Call-Me Card? Since then Mom's phoned me every day, no matter what—you know that. Yesterday, she never called, and the same today. Granny says not to worry, but I'm sick with worry."

"I'm sick, too." Arrow stood up. "Sick with anger. Your mom's run off with a gang of bikers. I thought she wanted to stay straight, that she was happy with me. Obviously, I was wrong."

The outside door banged. Into the school came Candy. "We're late leaving," she said to Arrow. "Squire's flipping his wig."

"I'll be right there."

Candy looked at Marie. "Are you a friend of Arrow's?"

"Not a chance!"

"We used to be friends," Arrow said, sounding sullen. "This girl's mother is the woman who ditched me."

"Really?" Candy looked at Marie with interest. "I think your mom made a mistake. Arrow's cool."

"Mom *didn't* ditch him," Marie cried. "Something terrible has happened—maybe because of Arrow!"

Candy looked at him. "Melody said I'd find Liz in the schoolhouse. Where is she?"

"I don't know," Arrow replied. "Let's get going."

The outside door banged as Arrow and Candy left the school. Immediately, I climbed out of the barrel and hurried over to Marie. Her eyes were bleary with tears. As I introduced myself, Aunt Melody came in from the storm.

"This is Marie," I said. "She lives in Willow Bunch with her grandmother. Her mom is Arrow's missing girl-friend."

"You poor kid. I do hope you'll find her."

"We're travelling with Arrow," I explained to Marie. Quickly, I outlined our story. "Listen, Marie, what do you think happened to your mom?"

"I don't know," she replied. "I keep trying to blame Arrow, but he was always nice until today. If he's not responsible, who is? And where's my mom?"

"You don't usually live with her?"

Marie shook her head. "She moved to Regina, where she helped Arrow run their business. I stayed in Willow Bunch, to be with my grandmother, but I visit Mom on weekends." She looked at Aunt Melody. "Please, may I come with you? Arrow's the only link to my mom. If I can stay close to him, maybe I'll find out something. I just can't sit in Willow Bunch and do nothing!"

"Would it be okay, Aunt Melody?"

"I don't think so, Liz. How would Marie's grand-mother feel, if she didn't come home today?"

Marie looked disappointed, but said no more. Back outside, I looked at the sky. The storm had ended, leaving big puddles to reflect the sunshine bursting through. Marie walked with us to the parking lot, where Squire was impatiently pacing.

"The bus won't start," he fumed. "I'm going crazy!"

"What's wrong?" Aunt Melody said to Arrow, who was working under the hood.

"Nothing much," he replied. "It's a little problem that happens occasionally."

"Get on your cell phone," Squire told Arrow, "and find a mechanic to make the repairs."

"Forget it, Squire, I don't have a cell phone," Arrow replied. "I can't afford one. Besides, I've fixed this before. We'll be leaving soon."

"Soon? I want to leave *now*. It's a long drive to Wood Mountain."

"What's in Wood Mountain?" Aunt Melody inquired.

"The new lines of latitude and longitude meet close to Wood Mountain. It's down near the U.S. border."

"I'd like to go into Moose Jaw," Aunt Melody said.

"But why?" Squire protested. "We must reach the next coordinates as quickly as possible."

"I only agreed to join your expedition for a short time, Squire, perhaps as far as Moose Jaw. I think I'll go home to Winnipeg now, and take Liz with me. Things could get dangerous here."

Squire turned to me with pleading eyes. "Before you go, Liz, give me the password. Okay?"

I shook my head. "If I go, the password goes with me."

Squire grabbed Aunt Melody's hands. "Please, please. Don't leave, Melody. Hey, there's no danger. Everything's fine!"

I nodded my agreement. "Squire's right, Aunt Melody. There's no risk at all. Besides, I've been learning all kinds of things. This expedition is like a computer camp—Squire's been teaching me the laptop. Right, Squire?"

"Yes, yes! Liz is an excellent student. I'd hate to lose her."

"Well, okay," Aunt Melody said. "I must admit this trip is proving to be fun. One thing I'm enjoying is the photography. I've already captured some magnificent vistas."

"Your pictures are excellent, Melody." Squire beamed at her. "I'm so pleased about your decision."

"But there's one condition. Tonight we stay in Moose Jaw."

"But, Melody—"

"Candy wants to get home, and there are things I want to see, like Mac the Moose and the Diamond Dogs."

"What's that? Some kind of rock group?"

"In addition, I plan to sleep tonight in a bed—not in a field. My back is killing me, so we'll find a nice motel. Mr. Smollett has kindly agreed to the extra expense."

"That's correct," Smollett said. He was studying a highway map. "Route 2 is the best way to Wood Mountain. Too bad we won't be going through Gravelbourg— my Uncle Patrick lives there, in a seniors' residence. I'd have enjoyed seeing him."

"There's no time for side trips," Squire fumed. "I'm in a hurry!"

As the driver from Willow Bunch beeped her horn, calling the kids for the return journey, I gave Marie a good-luck hug.

"We'll keep an eye on Arrow," I promised. "Give me your phone number, and I'll call with any news."

Marie scribbled the information on a scrap of paper. "Thanks for being so kind," she said quietly. A tear rolled down her cheek. "Something terrible has happened to Mom—I just know it."

Giving me a small smile, Marie climbed into the school bus. As it drove away, I felt a bony hand grip my elbow. Turning, I saw Smollett.

"A word with you," he hissed.

Smollett led me away from the bus. "I want some information, and I'm prepared to pay for it. I'm a wealthy man."

I didn't say anything.

Smollett stared into my eyes. "I want to know the secret password." He showed me a thick wad of money. "This is yours, in return for the password."

I shook my head. "No way, Mr. Smollett."

7

Mac the Moose was taller than a house. I stood under his bulky shadow, grinning for Aunt Melody's camera. The giant mascot of "The Friendly City" was high on her must-see list.

Nearby was a busy tourist bureau, and picnic tables where the others sat talking. As Aunt Melody went into the bureau, Candy joined me beside the huge moose.

"It's nice to be back in my home town," she said. "But I'll miss you guys."

"Why don't you stay with us? Your meals are scrumptious."

"I just suggested that to Squire and Smollett.

They're discussing it."

I looked at the men, arguing at a picnic table. "Smollett sure likes you, eh?"

"He's not my type."

I watched Candy light up another cigarette. "When did you start smoking?"

"Back in elementary school. Nicking out was the cool thing, you know? I strongly believed I wouldn't become addicted, but I did." She shrugged, then sucked smoke deep into her lungs. "People say smokers get bronchitis and asthma," she said, coughing, "but it won't happen to me. I was born lucky. I've done plenty and survived. Like, I've jumped from an airplane. Just for the thrill."

"With a parachute, I hope!"

Candy laughed. "Of course."

Squire appeared beside us. "Good news, Candy! I'm here to offer you the job of chief cook and bottle washer for our expedition."

Candy threw her arms around Squire. "You're wonderful!"

As Squire beamed, Smollett approached with a handful of cash. "Here's your first pay, Candy."

"Wow!" She also hugged Smollett, who grinned.

Aunt Melody joined us. She was clutching a stack of tourist brochures. "We're in luck. The local baseball team has a double-header starting late this afternoon. It's Prairie League action—this should be good!"

"I just got paid," Candy said. "I'll go with you."

"What about your exams?" I asked Aunt Melody.

"I need a break from studying."

"I'll go, too," Smollett said. "Then I'll treat every-one to supper at Pizza Hut."

Squire waved his hand. "I'll pass on the baseball. I'm staying at the motel to watch TV."

As the men walked away, Candy lit another ciga-rette. Then she looked at my aunt. "Melody, may I ask your advice?"

"Certainly."

"It's about Arrow." Candy glanced at a picnic table where Arrow faced the blue sky, soaking up UV rays. The dark skin of his face and bare chest glowed under the hot sun. "I think I'm falling in love."

"Oh, Candy. I don't know if that's a good idea."

Her eyes filled with tears. "Arrow's the first nice guy I've ever met, Melody. I can't bear the thought of never seeing him again."

"But he's got a girlfriend."

"Some friend!" Candy dragged on her cancer stick. "She ran off with a bunch of bikers from the States. That's not very loyal."

"Nobody knows that for sure about Teresa," I pointed out. "Maybe she was abducted or something."

Candy shook her head. "Arrow needs a good woman, and I'm the one."

*   *   *

Later, we checked out a local resort, the ultra-luxurious Temple Gardens with its famous mineral-water pool, four storeys in the sky. Then we walked to Ross Wells Park, home stadium of the Moose Jaw Diamond Dogs. The local favourites were set to battle the Dakota Rattlers, and fans were buzzing with excitement as they lined up for tickets.

"I should be a sports reporter," I said to Arrow, interrupting his conversation with Candy. "It's so exciting to be here!"

Squire had remained at the motel, but Smollett was with us. He kept trying to chat with Candy, but her attention was focused on Arrow. "Tell me something," Smollett said to them. "What's your opinion of this expedition? What kind of treasure are we searching for?"

Candy shrugged. "Who cares? I've got a job, and that's what counts."

"I agree," Arrow said. "My only goal is to forget being betrayed by Teresa."

Candy smiled at him. "Right now is the best time to start." She linked her arm through Arrow's and we followed them inside. The sun-bathed park was festive, with thousands in the stands. A mascot in a Diamond Dogs uniform entertained the crowd while the red dirt of the infield was given a final raking. Then, to loud cries from the stands, the teams appeared.

The words of "The Star-Spangled Banner" echoed off the outfield wall as the American players solemnly sang along, caps over their hearts. "A great song," I whispered to Aunt Melody as the anthem ended and "O Canada" began. "It's right up there with ours."

The first batter for the Diamond Dogs sliced a single into left field. Moments later, the next hit went over the wall. I leapt up and performed a victory dance while screaming, "We're number one! We're number one!"

The smoking bats of the Diamond Dogs soon drove

the Rattlers' pitcher to the showers, and his replacement didn't last long either. "The Rattlers are getting mighty rattled," I said to Aunt Melody with a laugh. The crowd chanted encouragement as their favourites stepped to the plate: *Mark, Mark, out of the park*, they cried, and *Mac, Mac, give it a smack*!

"I'm going to try for an autograph," I said to Aunt Melody, scuttling down the concrete stairs to the Dogs' dugout. Several players were signing autographs, and I joined the line. When I turned around, was I ever surprised! Marie was walking towards me, wearing a backpack.

"Marie! How'd you get here?"

"Our school bus driver has Diamond Dogs season tickets. She gave me a lift to the game. Your aunt said she wanted to see the Diamond Dogs, and I knew about today's double-header." She looked at me with those piercing blue eyes. "Liz, I have to go with you. Please get your aunt to say yes! I've got to stick close to Arrow. He's my only chance to find Mom."

"Okay, I'll ask Aunt Melody. But what about your granny?"

"She doesn't know I'm here. When your aunt gives permission, I'll phone Granny. She won't mind. She's worried, too."

Climbing the stands, we joined the others. Aunt Melody was surprised, but agreed to phone Marie's grandmother. She went in search of a pay phone, leaving us to watch the game. Out of the corner of my eye, I looked at Arrow and Candy, wondering how they felt about Marie's sudden appearance.

When Aunt Melody returned, she was smiling.

"You can stay with us, Marie, but only until we reach Willow Bunch. Your grandmother says it's not far from Wood Mountain."

I high-fived Marie. "Excellent!"

"I enjoyed talking to your grandmother," Aunt Melody said. "She thinks joining our expedition may keep you from worrying too much about your mother."

I looked at Marie. "Has your granny called the police?"

"Yes. To the cops, Mom is now a missing person file. That's not good enough for me."

"Got a picture of your mom?"

"Nope, but I wish I did. I miss her laughter." Marie sighed. "Liz, I brought something special to show you." She took a colourful woollen sash from her backpack; standing up, she wrapped the sash around her waist and knotted it. "Granny made this for me. The colours in the sash represent the four directions, like in a compass."

"It's beautiful."

"My heritage is Métis," Marie said proudly. "The sash is a symbol of our self-esteem. Long ago, all Métis wore the sash. Far from home, out on the prairie, it solved many problems. For example, the sash worked as a bridle in an emergency."

"What does Métis mean?"

"It's a French word meaning *a child of two races*. During the fur trade, men came from France and married Native women. The children of these marriages were the original Métis. They lived in the Red River Colony in the early 1800s."

"I'd love to meet your granny, Marie."

"I hope you will. But first, I've got to find my mom!"

"You will, Marie. I'm sure of it."

* * *

We left after the first game—Aunt Melody felt guilty about not studying, and the rest of us were anticipating a big feed at Pizza Hut!

Outside the stadium, Aunt Melody flagged a passing cab. "I'm going back to the motel to hit the books. I'll see you guys later."

Aunt Melody gave me a smile as the taxi whisked her away. The rest of us climbed inside the *Mañana Banana,* and it puttered through the leafy streets towards downtown Moose Jaw.

"Every community seems to have a war memorial," I said to Marie, as we passed a tribute to the city's fallen. "All those dead soldiers—it's so sad."

I looked at Candy, who was chattering brightly to Arrow about baseball. "She's after Arrow," I whispered to Marie. "But I can't tell if he's interested. Squire and Smollett have given Candy a job as expedition cook."

"Arrow looks so depressed. He's missing my mom," Marie said sadly.

"So are you, eh?"

"Yeah."

Trying to distract Marie from her blues, I got her talking about the unusual artistry in downtown Moose Jaw. On many brick walls, giant murals showed prairie history. Earlier, we'd seen pioneers threshing grain in golden fields, a long-ago baseball game, and the coming of the railroad.

"Look at the boy playing hockey," Marie said. "No helmets back then."

"See the number nine on his sweater? I bet that's Gordie Howe. He learned his hockey in Saskatchewan."

Smollett pointed at a tall tower with an iron clock. "That train station was built in the days of steam. You've probably heard of Al Capone, the Chicago gangster. The Soo Line from Chicago connects straight to Moose Jaw. There are plenty of rumours about Capone's gang heading north when things got too hot in Chicago. People say they hid under the streets of Moose Jaw."

"That's impossible," I said, "unless they were gophers."

"Yeah," Marie added, "little prairie dogs in mobster suits, carrying machine guns."

Smollett refused to smile. "Long ago," he lectured sternly, "secret tunnels were built under the city. People lived down there—gangsters, gamblers, fugitives from justice."

"Didn't the police find out?"

"Sure, but the chief was crooked—he was on the take. The tunnels were kept secret until the chief got busted. Then the scheme ended, real fast. No more gangsters, no more gambling."

Arrow said, "I heard you can visit those tunnels."

"Yes," Smollett replied. "I've taken the tour."

"Wow," I exclaimed. "Let's go see them!"

To my surprise, Smollett's brittle face cracked in a

brief smile. "I'm glad you're interested in history—good for you! Find a parking place, Arrow. The entrance to the tunnels is at the next corner."

* * *

We parked in the heart of historic Moose Jaw. Many buildings were brick two-storeys with flat roofs. Windows and doorways were arched in red brick. A sign read OK FOODS OK. Across a dusty parking lot, a faded advertisement on an old building invited us to visit THE BLUE STORE MEN'S WEAR.

At the tunnel entrance, Candy said goodbye to us. "I've got errands to run before we leave Moose Jaw." She kissed Arrow's cheek. "See you later, handsome."

As I exchanged a glance with Marie, Smollett gave Candy a sulky look. "What about our meal at Pizza Hut?"

"I'm not hungry."

"I confess I'm disappointed, Candy."

"Another time, okay?"

As Candy hurried away, we entered a building where a sign said TUNNELS OF LITTLE CHICAGO. While Smollett purchased tickets, Marie and I checked out the gift shop with Arrow. Other tourists joined us, and then we were escorted into the tunnels.

The history was explained by a friendly guide as she took us along dusty, narrow passages where bare lightbulbs fought the gloom. The tunnels were narrow but high, so we didn't need to stoop. "The CPR brought workers from China to help construct the railway," she said, her words echoing between the stone walls. "The

Chinese workers built these tunnels to hide from racist thugs in the streets. Most of Moose Jaw's Chinese restaurants were connected by the tunnels."

We entered a large room with tables and chairs. "Later on, others discovered the tunnels," the guide explained. "Some people actually lived down here." Light from a fringed lamp shone on a brocade sofa, where a pistol rested on a pillow. "These tunnels were the perfect hideout for gamblers and gangsters. That's why we named our attraction Little Chicago."

As we entered a dark shaft with wooden walls, our guide clanged a bell that hung from the ceiling. "This bell warned of potential danger. The moment it rang, people escaped into hiding." She touched the wall, and an invisible door swung open. "Another entrance to the tunnels," she said, gesturing into the darkness.

"Can we explore?" I asked.

"I'm afraid not," the guide said, closing the door. "Those tunnels are dangerous."

Arrow looked around the room. "This seems pretty safe."

"Yes, it was fixed up for tourists to visit. But many tunnels remain undeveloped. They're dark, and full of rubble and fallen timbers."

"Too bad," Arrow said to me. "Those old tunnels sound fascinating."

Back outside, we squinted in the light. "I'm so hungry," I said. "Where's Pizza Hut?"

Smollett's reply was interrupted by a woman from the tour. "My husband and I are visitors ourselves," she told us. "Last night on River Street, we had Chinese food. It was marvellous—you simply *must* eat there."

"Shall we?" Smollett asked, and everyone nodded in agreement.

"Wasn't that a great tour?" the woman's husband remarked. "Our friend Linda grew up in Moose Jaw. She told us there are *miles* of tunnels under the city, and many are still used as secret passages."

Saying goodbye, we walked a few blocks to the restaurant on River. In the nearby rail yards, boxcars crashed together as a freight train was assembled. "My brother, Tom, would love this place," I told Marie. "He's a train freak. Because I'm on this trip, Tom gets the next one. He's been invited to Vancouver to visit my grandparents—he's going there by train."

"That sounds like fun!"

The twilight sky was painted in pastels. A bright neon dragon beckoned to us from the restaurant, where lights glowed warmly inside. Candles flickered on the tables, making a cozy scene.

"Hey," I exclaimed, "there's Candy!"

She sat alone at a booth, sipping from a china teacup. As we entered the restaurant, she looked up in surprise. "You were going to Pizza Hut."

Smollett explained about the couple's recommendation. "I thought you weren't hungry," Arrow said as we joined Candy.

"I'm not," she replied. "A friend of mine named Chelsea lives in this neighbourhood. She's supposed to meet me here, to return some clothes I loaned her." Candy glanced at a clock on the wall. "Chelsea's late—I think I'll split. I've got plenty of errands before we leave town. If Chelsea shows up, please say I'll phone her later tonight."

"What does she look like?" I asked.

"Blonde hair and pretty eyes. You'll recognize Chelsea easily—she'll be the one carrying an armload of my clothes!"

"Don't go yet," Smollett said. "Stay and keep us company."

Candy rose to go. "Some other time. I'm in a hurry."

"Hey, who's paying the bills on this trip? Do you still want the job of cook?"

"Yes," Candy replied meekly.

"Then you'll join us for some Chinese food."

The waiter appeared through a door; I could see a long passage that led to the kitchen. We argued over the menu, then settled back in hungry anticipation. I'd convinced the others to include my personal favourite, Seven Treasure Chicken, and I was ready, willing, and able to eat.

"About those bikers at Teresa's bar," I said to Arrow. "Did you get a description from the bartender?"

"Sure. They had leather jackets, that kind of stuff."

"Was there a name on the jackets?"

"Yes—something creepy." Arrow thought for a moment. "Death Machine. That was the gang's name."

I exchanged a glance with Marie. "Those same bikers torched the barn and gunned down Blind Pew," I told her. Then I looked at Arrow. "Did the bartender describe any of those bikers? Was there a strange-looking one?"

"Yes, as a matter of fact. This one guy—"

"Had a tattoo of a spider's web, all over his shaved head and his neck. Right?"

Arrow stared at me. "How did you know?"

Smollett's eyes were also fixed on me. "That guy

sounds really weird."

"His name is Tarantula," I told them.

At that moment, the kitchen door opened and a man stepped out. I expected to see our waiter carrying steaming plates of food, but it wasn't him.

Instead, I saw Tarantula—the biker with the spider's web tattoo!

8

Arrow yelled in surprise. "Hey! That's him!" He leapt up. "Come back here!"

Smollett also jumped up, but lost his balance. He stumbled over a chair, and fell into Arrow's path. They crashed together to the ground, both yelling.

The biker disappeared through the kitchen door.

Arrow was getting up—but clumsy Smollett tripped again and they fell in a tangle of arms and legs, both cursing. Desperately, I ran down the passage to the kitchen, where I saw a chef leaning over a big stove. Someone else was washing dishes, and our waiter was placing chopsticks on a tray. But the biker was nowhere in sight. There was no hiding place, and the only window was barred. The back entrance was completely blocked by a truck delivering supplies; a man was wheeling a big sack out of the truck, but he wasn't the biker.

"He's gone," I said to Marie as she joined me.

The others crowded into the kitchen. "Where is he?" Arrow shouted at the waiter. "Where's that creep?"

Smollett pulled him back. "Take it easy." After Arrow calmed down, Smollett questioned the waiter and the others, but they claimed to have seen nothing.

We returned to the table. "What's going on?" Arrow said. "That's got to be the biker who was at Teresa's bar."

"Mom's his prisoner," Marie exclaimed. "Can't you understand that, Arrow? You *must* help me find Mom!"

"You're right, maybe I should. But then again, she left that note—saying not to look for her." Arrow shook his head, looking bewildered. "I don't know what to think."

Candy moved close to him. "You want some advice from a woman? You've been hurt, Arrow. You've been abandoned. It's time to think of your own needs."

"Yeah, maybe you're right."

"Find a woman who will truly appreciate you." Candy brushed Arrow's cheek with a kiss. "I've got errands to run." She stood up. "I'll meet you back here for a ride. If you've gone, I'll grab a taxi to the motel."

Candy left the restaurant. I was worried for her, but that didn't stop me from helping gobble down the delicious, nutritious, and totally toothsome feast. "Thanks, Mr. Smollett," I mumbled around a mouthful of sweet and sour. "Dis ish shimply great."

He didn't respond; a faraway look was in his eyes. "You haven't touched a bite," Marie said.

"Not hungry," Smollett replied, standing up. At the cash register, he paid the bill, then walked away into the night.

"He's a strange guy," Arrow said, as the three of us left the restaurant a few minutes later. "He can be really stingy about money, but sometimes really generous."

"Maybe he's afraid of being cheated," Marie suggested.

"Sometimes I feel cheated by life," Arrow said, shaking his head unhappily. "Listen, Marie, I know it hurts about your mom—but it's true. She's abandoned both of us. Now life must go on."

"But what if she's been kidnapped? I wish you'd help me to find Mom. She really cares for you, Arrow. She'd never walk out on you."

He shook his head. "By now Teresa is in Vancouver or somewhere, hanging out with her new-found biker pals. She's finished with me."

Marie said nothing more. At the *Mañana Banana*, she slumped into a seat, still not speaking. Arrow turned the key and the engine growled, but it wouldn't start.

"Not more trouble," he groaned.

The hood creaked open—steam rose in the air. "This'll take a while," Arrow said with a sigh, handing us some coins. "Go back to that restaurant for a Coke. I'll pick you up there."

* * *

Sitting in the window of the restaurant, we watched the changing lights of the neon dragon. After the waiter took our order, I looked at Marie. "Does your dad live in Saskatchewan?"

"He died when I was two."

"I'm really sorry, Marie. What do you think he was like?"

"Granny says he was kind, and curious." She beamed. "Daddy was a poet! I found some romantic stuff he wrote my mom. It was so sweet."

The waiter arrived with our drinks. As he returned to the kitchen, I said to Marie, "I can't believe Arrow would hurt your mom."

"You're right, Liz." Marie sighed. "I had to blame someone, so I chose Arrow. But I was wrong." She fiddled with the candle on our table. "I'm sure those bikers abducted Mom. But where is she?"

I thought for a minute. "Remember how the guide said the tunnels connected most Chinese restaurants in Moose Jaw? This is a really old building. What if there's a tunnel under here?"

Marie's blue eyes glowed with excitement. "You think that's how the biker escaped?"

I nodded. "Maybe there's a secret panel in the corridor that leads to the kitchen—let's go see." I picked up the candle. "This may be useful."

We went into the corridor. A swinging door connected to the kitchen; I could hear voices and the sizzle of cooking. "I watched how the tour guide opened that secret door," I whispered to Marie. Slowly, I moved along the wall, reaching up. "She found a catch, near the ceiling."

"Hurry, Liz! Someone may come."

"Okay, I'll just . . . Hey! I've found something."

With a *pop*! of escaping air, a section of the wall swung open. Waiting for us was a cold, dark tunnel. I turned to Marie, whose eyes were huge. "This could lead us to Tarantula. Should we chance it?"

"Those bikers scare me, but maybe they've got Mom. Let's go."

* * *

The tunnel smelled musty. Closing the secret panel, we stood together in the light of the candle. "Let's keep moving," I whispered, trying to sound courageous.

Marie didn't speak. Her eyes were enormous. I heard the thundering of her heart, or maybe it was my own. Holding the candle in front, I led the way. The flickering light showed bare pipes above us; junk was scattered underfoot. We moved slowly, searching the gloom for hazards.

"I hope there aren't any rats," I whispered.

Marie didn't reply. Despite the cold, she was sweating, and her eyes darted about fearfully.

Ahead, we saw a dark doorway. I held the candle higher, trying to see past the shattered door hanging from its hinges. We moved closer. "It's some kind of room," I whispered. "The roof must have collapsed— the room's full of earth and broken timbers."

"I see cards on the floor. Maybe people gambled here."

"You're right. Dead gamblers could be under that mess."

"Liz, let's go. I'm scared."

We found our way around a corner. Light glowed from above, showing a ladder. Quickly we climbed it, emerging into a dark corridor. Thin strips of light slanted into the darkness from splits in the corridor's wooden wall.

Squinting through the wall, I looked into a large commercial garage. There were tools on several workbenches. I saw a number of motorcycles, plus one ancient pickup truck. There were chairs and a TV set and a battered sofa; on the wall was a Harley-Davidson poster with the words *One With the Wind*.

The biker with the spider's web tattoo was leaning over a sidecar attached to his motorcycle. Beside him was the blonde woman who'd gunned down Blind Pew. She was talking to a second woman, who sat in the sidecar. I couldn't hear their words.

"That's my mom!"

"Oh, Marie. We've found her!"

She had the same face and eyes as Marie, but her hair was red. "Do you recognize that leather jacket she's wearing? Is it hers?"

"I don't think so." Marie turned to me. "Mom's their prisoner! I've got to save her." She knelt down. "The wall's broken at the bottom—there's just enough room to squeeze through. I've got to free her."

"Don't, Marie! You're asking for big trouble."

"Mom and Granny are all I've got." Marie stuck her head through the opening. Then she stopped. For a moment she didn't move, and I got worried.

"Are you okay?" I whispered.

Crawling backwards, Marie looked up at me. Tears

were streaming down her face. "Liz, I can't," she sobbed. "I'm too scared."

"I don't blame you," I said, helping her to stand. Suddenly, the noise of motorcycle engines thundered from the garage. As the bikers powered their motors, a heavy door rolled up.

The blonde woman walked to a light switch beside a small outside door. The garage fell dark except for the brilliance of the motorcycle headlights. I saw the woman climb on behind another biker, then the air shook as the big machines roared out of the garage.

Slowly, the big door descended. Now the only light came from our candle. "Are you okay, Marie?"

"Liz, we've got to search that garage! Maybe there's something they left, a map or something. Otherwise, how will I find my mom?"

"Okay—let's look for a way in." We followed the candle's orange glow along the dark corridor. At the end was a door. Stepping into the garage near the pickup truck, we closed the door behind us. The light of our candle showed a few dim shapes in the large, gloomy garage.

"Let's turn on the lights," Marie suggested.

At that moment, I heard a sound. I swung towards the small outside door—it was opening!

*   *   *

With impossible speed, we dove into hiding behind the old pickup. The darkness was cut by a flashlight beam. Leaning around the tire that sheltered me, I saw a dark shape follow the ray of light to a workbench in the corner. It was the blonde biker.

She picked up a tote bag. Inside, I glimpsed something black. Moments later, the flashlight went off, and I saw the biker's silhouette slip through the doorway into the night. Slowly, I released a very deep breath, then turned in Marie's direction.

"We'd better get help."

"Yes." Her voice trembled.

Outside, we saw telephone poles and a large parking lot with a few cars. There was no sign of the bikers. From the distance came the banging of rail cars. The moon lit the words THE BLUE STORE MEN'S WEAR on the side of a brick building.

"We're not far from Arrow! Let's go tell him what happened."

But at Main Street we received an unpleasant surprise. The *Mañana Banana* had disappeared.

*　　*　　*

Marie looked at me. "What'll we do now?"

"We'd better get a taxi to the motel."

"Liz, I feel so terrible. If I'd crawled through that opening, I could have saved my mom."

"Not necessarily, Marie."

She ran both hands through her long hair, then looked at me with sorrowful eyes. "I'm a coward, Liz."

"Of course you're not. The tunnels were super scary, but you got through them."

"That narrow little opening freaked me." Her eyes widened at the memory. "It felt like a trap."

"I think you're really brave, Marie."

"We'd better tell the police what happened."

"You're right. But first, let's take a taxi to the motel, so the others know we're okay."

We reached the motel just as another taxi pulled away. I paid our driver, and we got out. The parking lot was crowded with cars; lights glowed from windows where people sat, watching television.

Arrow and Candy stood beside the *Mañana Banana*, talking in low voices. Candy's hair was messy; I glanced at Arrow, wondering if they'd been kissing. As we approached, they stepped away from each other.

Arrow was definitely annoyed with us. "Where have you girls been? After I got the bus fixed, I went to the restaurant. But you'd disappeared. I drove all over, looking for you. I only just arrived back here. I've been worried sick!"

"Guess what, Arrow," Marie exclaimed. "We saw Mom! She's not in Vancouver—she's right here in Moose Jaw! Or, at least, she was half an hour ago."

Arrow was astonished by the news, and so was Candy. They both stared at Marie. "What are you talking about?" Arrow demanded.

As Marie told her story, his face turned scornful. "That proves it. Teresa ran away with those bikers, just like I said."

"It's not true," Marie cried. "Mom's their prisoner! Arrow, please help me find her!"

As he hesitated, Candy looked at him. "She betrayed your dreams, Arrow. Do you really want Teresa back?"

"I . . . No, I guess not."

Candy touched his arm. "I'd respect you, Arrow. I'd never abandon you."

"Well . . ."

I looked at my watch. "It's getting really late, and we still have to find the police station. They'll want to know what happened."

"What will you say?" Candy asked. "That Teresa's joined a motorcycle gang?"

"That's not true," Marie replied indignantly. "Mom would never abandon Arrow." She looked at him with tearful eyes. "You should believe in Mom, like I do."

"You're right, Marie. Maybe I . . ."

"Excuse the interruption," Candy said, "but Liz is right—the police must be notified. Let's go inside and phone them."

* * *

Soon after, an officer arrived to hear our story. We stood outside with him in the warm air, discussing the events downtown. Aunt Melody had joined us, but Smollett and Squire were asleep.

From the officer we learned that the garage was the clubhouse for a Moose Jaw motorcycle gang. "They're out of town this weekend," he said, "so maybe those American bikers borrowed their meeting place. We'll make some inquiries."

Next morning, we ate McMuffins at McDonald's. Aunt Melody was seriously considering taking me on the next flight home to Winnipeg, but fortunately Squire and I were able to convince her otherwise.

Smollett returned from a pay phone, where he'd

called his office for messages. "I've got bad news, Squire," he said. "We'll have a detour today. We're going to Gravelbourg."

"But *why?*"

"My Uncle Patrick lives in a seniors' residence in Gravelbourg. Apparently he's very ill, and is asking for me."

"You poor man," Candy said. "What upsetting news."

To his credit, Squire agreed to the detour without further discussion. As we headed south on Highway 2, Marie gazed out at the green land all around stretching to the horizon. "It's as big as the sky out there. Mom could be anywhere."

Candy leaned over to squeeze her hand. "I'm sure you'll get her back, Marie." She looked at Squire, snoring in the only comfortable chair. "Look at that guy! He does nothing but sleep." Searching in her backpack, she found a cassette and slipped it into the stereo. "I hope this heavy metal doesn't disturb Squire's slumbers."

As the music blasted, Squire woke up fast. Snorting and groaning, he looked around with bleary eyes. Grinning, Candy went into the WC and closed the door. Emerging a few minutes later, she washed her hands and then dropped the towel in the laundry hamper.

Suddenly, Marie leapt up. "Stop the bus," she cried at Arrow. "Please!"

The bus pulled over. We all watched Marie run back to a dusty telephone pole. "Liz, come quickly," she called.

I jumped off the bus. The sun burned down hot. A big combine rolled past along the highway as I hurried to Marie. She'd pulled a faded poster off the telephone pole. On it was a singer, her hair streaked many colours. I looked at the date; the singer's gig had been several months earlier.

"This is my mom! It's an omen we'll find her."

"Your mom—wow. I hardly recognize her."

"I'm keeping this picture," Marie said, tearing it out of the poster.

We hurried back to the bus. As it pulled onto the highway, I studied the picture of Marie's mother. "You've got her eyes, and those beautiful cheekbones. But last night in the garage, her hair was red."

"Mom's always dying her hair. She wants to pass as white."

"How come?"

"She's ashamed."

"Of what?"

"Lots of Métis are that way—they've been brain-washed to feel ashamed of our culture."

"What do you mean?"

"You've heard of Louis Riel? He was our leader and our hero. He and other Métis tried to protect our land and our rights when the government took everything away." Marie looked directly at me with those intense blue eyes. "They hanged Riel and then called us rebels. It was a lie, but some people still believe it."

"I bet your granny doesn't."

"You're so right! She's the proudest Métis to ever walk this land."

Soon after, we left Highway 2 enroute to Gravelbourg.

"While we're there," Candy said to Squire, "I'll get some supplies."

"What kind of food? *Pâté de fois gras*?"

"Huh?"

"Gravelbourg is a French community—everyone knows that." Squire scowled. "I was just making a joke."

"Oh, I see," Candy said. "Very amusing, Squire."

As we approached Gravelbourg, Aunt Melody leaned close to the window. "Do my eyes deceive me? I see a cathedral, as big as one in Montreal or Paris. In the middle of the prairie?"

The twin bell towers of the cathedral rose magnificently into the sky; the only thing higher was the town's water tower. "OUR LADY OF ASSUMPTION," Aunt Melody read from a large sign outside the cathedral. "The name's also in French, but mine's rusty."

"*LA CATHÉDRALE NOTRE DAME DE L'ASSOMPTION*," Marie read out in perfectly accented French.

"You speak the language?"

Marie smiled at Aunt Melody. "*Bien sûr*."

"Hey, look at the street sign," I said. "*Rue* Main Street. Everything's bilingual!"

Words on a bank said *CAISSE POPULAIRE*; a store's sign offered *VIANDES*—MEATS and *LÉGUMES*—VEGETABLES. I leaned close to the window, staring at the pleasant streets as Arrow followed Smollett's directions to his uncle's residence. He rushed inside, but minutes later emerged with a big smile on his face.

"Uncle Patrick is fine! He's not sick or anything."

"But what about the message?" Candy asked.

"Who cares?" Smollett looked at his watch. "We're really late for lunch, so let's eat. After that I may visit my uncle for a while."

"But," Squire objected, "what about Wood Mountain? We must find those coordinates!"

"Do you want lunch?" Smollett asked him.

"Of course."

"Who's buying?"

Squire scowled. "You, I guess."

"If I'm paying the bills, I get to visit my uncle. Do you understand?"

"You bore me," Squire muttered, but he said no more.

On *rue* Main Street, Arrow stopped the bus outside a restaurant with stone walls. "I feel as if I'm a tourist in Quebec," Aunt Melody said. "This will be a wonderful lunch."

"I'll join you inside," Candy said. "First, I'm having a cigarette."

The café was cool and dark. Light splashed down on tables where people were speaking both French and English as they lunched together. Happily, our waiter was young and cute, and the food was great.

While eating lasagna, garlic toast, and Greek salad, we watched music videos on a large screen. "My mom wants to make a video," Marie said. "Then she'd get it broadcast on Country Music Television, and maybe get her big break. But videos cost a lot of money to make."

"Teresa's got a great voice," Arrow said. "But she'd hate being in the music industry. There are some tough people in that world. Teresa's so gentle—those sharks would destroy her."

"But she'd be a *star*," Marie protested. "She'd be famous everywhere. I'd be so proud."

Arrow smiled at her. "Aren't you proud already?"

"That's true," Marie admitted. "Oh, Arrow, where can she be?"

He shook his head sadly. "I just don't know."

Candy leaned her head against his shoulder. "I'd make your heart sing, Arrow. Just give me the chance."

"Forget it," he growled. "I'm a loser at love."

As Squire shovelled up lasagna, chunks fell to his plate. "You should be careful," I warned him. "Dropping food from your fork is bad luck."

"Stuff and nonsense! Superstitious twaddle."

"Okay, but you've been warned."

My heart beat faster as our waiter approached. His name was Joseph, and he had an awesome smile. Leaning close to Marie, I whispered, "I think I'm in love."

"Me, too."

"What's the history of this town?" Aunt Melody asked Joseph.

"The Gravel family came with others from Quebec in 1906 to settle this area," he replied, while clearing our table.

"The cathedral is enormous. When was it built?"

"I'm not sure."

Squire interrupted their conversation. "The cathedral was constructed almost a century ago, following the arrival of the Sisters of Jesus and Mary. The

murals inside were painted by Father Charles Maillard." He stared at Joseph. "Do you attend that
cathedral, Joseph?"

"Yes, sir."

"Then you should know its history."

"Sure, but . . . "

Squire looked around the table. "Kids these days
don't want to learn anything. No wonder the country's
falling apart."

Joseph's handsome face turned red. He gave Squire
a dirty look and walked away. Someone else brought
our dessert, and Joseph wasn't around when we left the
restaurant. I was upset because I wanted to apologize
for Squire's boorish behaviour.

"Silly young pup," Squire said, blinking in the sunshine. "Did you tip him, Smollett?"

"Of course not. Never pay tax, never leave a tip.
That's my motto." He looked admiringly at Squire. "I
must say, your knowledge of local history is impressive."

"Didn't you look at the placemats on the table?
They tell the story of Gravelbourg."

Marie whispered in my ear, "What a jerk." I smiled
sadly at her; my mind was on Joseph.

Lighting a cigarette, Candy looked at Squire. "I've
heard you're a real brain with computers. Right?"

Squire beamed. "You bet! I'm the best."

"Then how come," Candy asked, puffing on her
smoke, "you're such a lunkhead about kids?"

Squire's mouth fell open. "A *lunkhead*?"

Candy nodded. "You were cruel to Joseph, and
you're condescending to Liz and Marie. Don't you respect young people, Squire?"

His face turned bright red. "I . . . I . . . "

"Because I've seen these girls exhibit more brain power than you'll ever assemble in that thick noggin of yours. Not to mention courage, searching those tunnels for Marie's mother." She wagged her finger under Squire's nose. "You should be ashamed."

Aunt Melody grinned at her. "Well said, Candy!" She turned to Squire, who was gasping for air like a stranded rock cod. "By the way, cousin, have you phoned the RCMP in Regina? You were supposed to, after we got to Moose Jaw. Remember?"

Squire puffed himself up until he resembled an indignant hedgehog. "Of course."

"What did they say?"

"I'm to report again after Wood Mountain."

"Are you certain you spoke to them?"

"Absolutely!" Squire turned and climbed into the bus. Shaking her head, Candy lit another cigarette. "I need this," she said. "Squire gets on my nerves. All that braying, just like a donkey." She shrugged. "But who cares? I'm just along for the ride, and the chance to earn a few bucks." Candy winked at me. "Besides, Arrow is *really* cute, so that's a bonus."

Inside the bus, Arrow yelled angrily and slammed his fist against the steering wheel. "What's the problem?" Aunt Melody called to him.

"The bus won't start."

Squire exploded. "Great," he shouted. "One problem after another!"

Arrow opened the hood—steam rose into the sunshine. "It's dead as a doornail," he proclaimed. "If it weren't for bad luck, I wouldn't have any."

"The same problem as before?" Smollett asked.

"No, this is something different." Arrow leaned over the engine, examining it. "We'll need to find a garage. The *Banana* is seriously ill."

Smollett sighed deeply. "I guess I'm paying."

"Since we're delayed," Candy said, "I might as well buy more supplies." She held out her hand to Smollett. "I need money."

Smollett reluctantly passed over some bills. "At this rate, I'll soon be broke. But it's worth it, Candy, just breathing the same air as you." He turned to Squire. "While the bus is being repaired, we'll have a meeting—just the two of us. We must continue our discussion."

"Okay, but you already know my opinion."

* * *

At the garage we agreed on a departure time. Deciding to get her hair cut, Aunt Melody left us. Marie and I enjoyed being together, wandering around town. People were really friendly. "I'm looking for my mom," Marie explained to one lady, who abandoned her yard work for a chat. "This is her picture. Maybe you've seen her?"

"No, *chérie*," the lady said sadly. "How *triste*. I do hope you will succeed."

"*Merci bien*," Marie replied, smiling bravely.

We followed *Rue* Main Street to the cathedral. High above us were twin crosses, silhouetted against the evening sky. "We'll never make Wood Mountain tonight," I said.

Marie chuckled. "Squire will be fuming."

Beside the cathedral was a large brick house with white pillars. The grounds were extensive, with many trees and a tall flagpole. A ride-on mower was parked beside a large garage. "Nice place," I said. "I wonder who lives here."

A neon sign that said SNACK SHACK EATERY beckoned to us from down the street. "Let's get some fries," Marie suggested.

"Sounds good!"

The small eatery was in the middle of an enormous parking lot with a scattering of cars. "This lot was designed by an optimist," I joked. "I see they feature a Gravelburger. Now *that* would be hard on the teeth!"

Inside, a teenaged couple gabbed together. We placed our order, then Marie approached their table. "We're looking for my mom," she said, displaying her photo.

"Can't help you," the boy said.

"Sorry," his girlfriend added. "But good luck, eh?"

"Thanks," Marie replied quietly.

"I wish we had a picture of Tarantula," I said to her. "It would be something else to show people."

"I could do a drawing."

"That would be great!"

Marie asked for a placemat. On the back, she quickly sketched the biker and his spider's web tattoo. It was an excellent likeness. "That's amazing work, Marie."

"Thanks!"

She showed the drawing to the teenagers. To our astonishment, the girl nodded her head. "Yes, I saw him today. Here in Gravelbourg."

9

"I can't believe it!" Marie exclaimed.

"I was walking past the bishop's house today, and I saw a weird-looking guy at an upstairs window. Your drawing is a lot like him."

"You're talking about that big house beside the cathedral?" I said. "The local bishop lives there?"

"Yes, but right now he's in Rome."

"So the house is empty?"

She shook her head. "Nuns live across the street. Sister Rita moves into the bishop's house when he's away, to look after things."

Thanking the couple, we left the Snack Shack Eatery. "There's about an hour until sunset," Marie said, contemplating the sky.

"Feel like checking out the bishop's house?" I asked.

"Okay—I guess so."

"See the cathedral's bell towers?" I said. "From up there, we could look down into the bishop's house. We might spot that biker, or maybe your mom."

"Okay, let's try to get inside."

At the side door of the cathedral, I looked up at the enormous stone walls stretching towards the sky. "It must have taken forever to build this place."

"The door's unlocked," Marie said, pushing it open.

"People here really trust each other, eh? It's nice."

Inside, I was amazed by the beauty. Far above, I saw marble angels and stained-glass windows. Shafts of evening sunshine lit the pews with dappled colours. The words *SANCTUS SANCTUS SANCTUS* were far above the altar on a cream-coloured arch.

"No one's here," I whispered.

There was a hush in the vast space. Then I heard the echo of voices, far away in a hidden part of the cathedral. I looked at Marie; her eyes were wide.

The voices came closer. I saw a sudden shaft of light from a room, then heard a door close. The voices continued, too muffled to be understood.

"Come on," Marie whispered, beckoning me forward.

This part of the cathedral was very dark. We passed some flickering candles, then climbed a few steps into a murky space. Now the voices were closer; we crept towards light seeping under a door.

But then my foot caught on the carpet. I stumbled forward, reaching helplessly for support, and crashed to my knees. Immediately, the voices stopped.

As I stood up, rubbing pain away, the door opened. A nun stepped out; dark hair fringed her kindly face, and she wore glasses. "Yes, girls?" she said, carefully closing the door. "My name is Sister Rita. May I help you?"

"We're looking for my mom." Marie unfolded the picture. "This is her, only now she's a redhead."

"I'm sorry." Sister Rita's voice trembled as she spoke. "I can't help."

I showed her Marie's drawing of the biker. "Have you seen this guy, Sister Rita?"

Her eyes were wide. "You must leave now, girls. The cathedral is closing for the night."

"Sister Rita, please!" Stalling for time, I looked up at the enormous paintings that dominated the cathedral walls. "Who did those, Sister Rita?"

"The cathedral's first priest, Father Maillard." She led us towards the exit. "In the paintings, the model for Jesus was a young priest who'd just arrived in Gravelbourg from Quebec."

"That's really interesting, Sister Rita. Would you show us around?"

Her eyes flickered nervously. "I'm in a meeting. They're waiting for me."

"Okay," I said reluctantly. "But it's a beautiful place."

"Thank you," she replied quietly.

At the door, Sister Rita said to Marie, "May the Lord guide you to your mother." She touched our hands and murmured a blessing, then quickly closed the door.

"She's upset about something," Marie said.

"I agree. Listen, we never reached the bell towers. Want to try again?"

"I guess so."

We cautiously stepped back inside—light gleamed under the door where Sister Rita was attending her meeting. Across from us, a stained-glass window showed a sheaf of wheat; it glowed with the light from the sunset outside.

A train whistled somewhere, then silence returned to the cathedral. Using extreme caution, we tiptoed to the entrance to one of the bell towers. Stairs led up; we climbed slowly into the darkness.

Unfortunately, the stairs soon ended. In the ceiling above was a trap door impossible to reach. "We'd have to get through that trap door to climb higher in the bell tower." I looked at a nearby door. "Maybe we can find a ladder."

In search of one, we entered a large choir loft. I saw an organ, and chairs that faced the distant altar. Above us, on a large stained-glass window, a saint was being escorted to Heaven by angels with peacock-coloured wings. Peering outside through a section of orange glass, I saw orange trees and orange houses and orange grain elevators.

I glanced at my watch. "We'd better go."

"Liz, look!"

Far below us, Sister Rita was walking towards the altar. Kneeling, she began to pray. I turned to Marie. "What if she's there a long time?"

"Maybe . . ."

A hiss echoed through the silent cathedral. Sister Rita looked towards the sound. In a gloomy doorway, a hand was beckoning. In the darkness I couldn't see the person, only something red flashing from the hand. It was a spooky image.

Sister Rita prayed a moment longer, then crossed herself. Hurrying to the doorway where the hand had beckoned, she disappeared from sight.

* * *

Unable to climb higher in the bell tower, we gave up and left the cathedral. Outside, the sky was growing dark. "We're late meeting the others," I said, checking my watch again.

We hurried along *rue* Main Street, discussing Sister Rita. As we approached the bus, Squire was yelling at Candy. Spotting us, he said, "You're late, too! We agreed on a departure time. What's wrong with you?"

Saying nothing, we slunk onto the bus. As Candy began putting away the supplies, the engine purred into life. Arrow smiled at Smollett. "Thanks for the repairs."

"I had no choice."

I sat beside Aunt Melody. "Your hair cut looks nice."

"Thanks, Liz. Have you been exploring?"

I nodded. "There's lots to tell you."

The *Mañana Banana* rolled through the night, past the cathedral and the Snack Shack Eatery, then reached the junction of highways 43 and 58. As we turned south and left Gravelbourg behind, I looked at the horizon. The sky and land were both totally black, framing a golden glow that lingered after the sunset.

From somewhere, I heard the roar of motorcycles. Looking back to the junction, I saw headlights moving out of Gravelbourg in a pack. Heading east on 43, they were lost in the night.

* * *

Once again, we camped in a farmer's field. At dawn, I awoke in my sleeping bag with a sore back and a stiff neck. Sitting up, I put on my glasses. The sky was the colour of oyster shells; little birds with yellow throats flittered about.

We were at the top of a low hill. Candy, Aunt Melody, and Marie were all asleep. On the other side of the fire pit, the guys were noisily snoring. Beyond was the green land, so enormous and so empty of people. I saw a car leaving a distant farm, and a truck looking so small it was like a child's toy—otherwise, I felt completely alone in the world.

In a nearby field, I saw a little wooden church surrounded by wild grass; the arched windows and bell tower reminded me of a Christmas card. Curious, I crossed the dusty road towards the church, which seemed to be abandoned. A *screech!* sounded from above, where a hawk joyfully rode invisible air currents. Beside a rusty barbed-wire fence, yellow wildflowers tossed their heads in the wind.

An old padlock hung on the church's weathered door; through a cracked window, I saw empty chairs facing the altar. I thought of people coming here to worship. Where were they now?

In a far corner of the enormous churchyard, crosses

rose above the wild grass. The wind moaned in my ears as I made a path towards the graves. There were seven headstones, some of stone and others of wood. I read the names and long-ago dates, wondering about the people.

"Liz."

I jumped straight in the air. Whirling around, I saw Aunt Melody.

"Sorry," she said sheepishly. "I didn't mean to startle you. I came over to say good morning."

"These graves are so sad, Aunt Melody." I took her to a simple cross; burned into the wood was the name of a young mother who'd died in 1933. "See that other grave? She lost her twin babies, then a month later she died herself." I took off my glasses and brushed a hand across my eyes, feeling sad. "It's so tragic."

Aunt Melody patted my shoulder sympathetically. She looked at the horizon, where dark clouds were gathering. "Times have often been hard in Saskatchewan. Decades ago, the prairies suffered a terrible drought. There was grit everywhere—on people's clothing, in their eyes, and always on the wind. Finally the crops came back, but then a plague of grasshoppers descended on the fields and ate everything."

"Why did people come here? It sounds so difficult."

"They arrived with great hopes for their families. It must have been exciting, settling a new land. They couldn't have known such terrible hardships would come to them."

She looked at the crosses. "These babies died during the Depression, possibly of whooping cough. Back then, there was no government health care—people had to pay cash to see a doctor. Many parents couldn't afford to get medical help for their children or themselves."

Aunt Melody studied the graveyard. "After a lot of suffering, people banded together to help each other. That's what governments are for, Liz. Canada's medicare system was born in Saskatchewan—nobody wanted any more babies to die just because their parents lacked money."

Aunt Melody photographed the church against the sky, which had grown dark. A tongue of lightning flicked down to the earth; rain fell in sheets from faraway black clouds.

"I'm glad we came here, Aunt Melody. Maybe no one has visited this cemetery for a long time."

Back at the bus, we had Candy's delicious Saskatoon-berry pancakes for breakfast. Afterwards, we helped pack up the supplies and bury the campfire, then climbed into the bus.

As we journeyed south, I talked to Marie about the cemetery. In the distance, dust rose from a road. "Bikers," I said, "heading east." A few minutes later, a second pack of motorcycles appeared on the road before us. Quickly they approached, then roared past with engines thundering. Their licence plates were from Alberta.

We stopped for gas at Flintoft. As a mechanic checked under the hood, I asked him, "What's with all the bikers? Is there a convention or something?"

"Yup," he replied. "They have a big party every year at Assiniboia. It's this weekend. Bikers are coming from all over, including the States."

Marie looked at me. "I bet they took Mom there!"

She went straight to Squire, who was drinking a Dr. Pepper outside the gas station, and begged for a detour to Assiniboia. But he refused, and Aunt Melody supported his decision. "I promised your grandmother you'd be home soon."

"But Assiniboia's not far!"

"We have no proof your mother's there, Marie."

Candy stubbed out a cigarette. "Don't mess with bikers, Marie. They're dangerous."

"Okay," she reluctantly agreed. "But it's a rotten decision."

We climbed into the bus; above us, the skies were black. As the *Mañana Banana* returned to the road, Marie's sad eyes studied the picture she'd ripped from the poster. "I know I'll find Mom."

Candy asked to see it. "Red hair suits her better, but I like the jewellery. Your mom's got taste."

"That's what I used to think," Arrow said mournfully from the wheel. "But obviously she prefers bikers."

Further discussion was interrupted by a blast of white light, followed by the most enormous *bang!* I'd ever heard. "What was that?" I yelped.

"Thunder," Smollett replied. "Straight above."

Another flash of lightning and crash of thunder made me wince, and then torrents of rain cascaded across the windshield and down the windows. "I can't see the road," Arrow said, pulling over to the side.

Rain hammered the metal roof of the *Mañana Banana*. Huge quantities of water poured down the windows, blocking my view. As we waited out the storm, I thought of Sister Rita—her behaviour at the cathedral had been strange and troubling.

Finally, the storm weakened and Arrow returned to the road. South of the village of Wood Mountain, we entered a valley fringed by hills. "This is the Legare Valley," Marie said. "It's named for Jean-Louis Legare, one of my ancestors. He founded Willow Bunch, and provided food for Sitting Bull."

"The famous Sioux chief?" Smollett asked.

Marie nodded. "After the Battle of Little Big Horn, Sitting Bull escaped to Canada with his people. This valley became their home until eventually they returned to the States."

I looked up a hill, trying to picture Sioux warriors. "Hey," I said, as we rounded a corner, "there's a teepee!"

It was in a large field beside a small white building. A sign said WOOD MOUNTAIN POST HISTORIC PARK. "Let's go see," I exclaimed.

Predictably, Squire protested. But Smollett instructed Arrow to pull over, and moments later we stepped out beside the teepee. We were the only people around. To Squire's annoyance, Aunt Melody insisted on a group photograph, and took her time setting it up.

A woman came out of the building and offered to take the picture. She was wearing a uniform and cap; her blue eyes were pretty, and she had curly brown hair. "I'm Judy," she said. "Come and see the museum."

Inside the white building, a Union Jack dominated one wall. "Before Saskatchewan became a province," Judy explained, "this land was part of the Northwest Territories. The Mounted Police made their headquarters at this fort when Sitting Bull and his 5,000 Sioux were here. The Mounties came west to keep the peace, and the Sioux respected them. Everyone got along just fine."

Judy handed me a fur coat. "Try this on. It belonged to the Mounties."

"It's really heavy," I said, struggling into the coat.

"That's buffalo hide—perfect protection against wind and snow. In winter, this country gets mighty cold. I've heard stories of people snowed in for so long that they went crazy. Some were so hungry, they ate their shoe leather."

Squire looked at his watch, then at Judy. "We're looking for the grave of someone named Thompson."

"The former Mountie?"

"I think so. The letters *NWMP* are after his name."

"That's Jimmy. He was one of the original North West Mounted Police. Jimmy married Mary Hawk, one of Sitting Bull's people. They're buried on a hill just south of here."

"Excellent!" Squire's eyes gleamed. "We're getting closer and closer."

"If you'd like," Judy said, "I'll phone the people who own the land. It's private—you'll need their permission to visit the grave site."

"Thank you, Judy," Aunt Melody said. "We'd appreciate that."

After making the arrangements, Judy accompanied us outside. A school bus was approaching; on the side were the words RED COAT TRAIL SCHOOL DIVISION NO. 69. Kids stared at us from the windows as it stopped. "Another school tour," Judy said with a grin. "The rain's been keeping my mud vacuum busy today."

"Red Coat Trail," Aunt Melody said. "I saw that on a highway sign last night."

Judy nodded. "They call Highway 13 the Red Coat Trail. It follows the route taken by the Mounties who marched west in 1874."

Following Judy's directions, we soon reached a house and outbuildings set on a large acreage. Getting off the bus, we were greeted by a woman with greying hair and a merry smile. "I'm Nora," she said, removing her work gloves to shake hands. "I've been chopping wood, getting ready for next winter. You're looking for Jimmy, eh?" She pointed at a hill. "The cemetery is up there."

"May we look?" Aunt Melody asked.

"Why not? It's suddenly a popular place. Some biker came by recently, looking to find a grave in a remote location. I sent him up the hill to Jimmy's cemetery."

I glanced at Marie with excited eyes. "Was his motorcycle from California?" I asked Nora.

"I didn't notice." She pointed to bushes behind the woodpile. "Some of Jimmy and Mary's kids are buried out back—they lived here before us. People ask if I'm afraid of ghosts running around." She laughed heartily. "As if!"

"Have you been here long?"

"Quite a spell. My husband and I come from Palmer area. Heck, at Palmer it's so flat, you can see fifty miles to the lights of Assiniboia. At first, I found this valley like a prison, the hills and trees shutting me in. But I love it down here now. It's home." She pulled on her gloves. "Well, back to work."

After thanking her, we climbed the hill. Mosquitoes rose from the wet grass, feasting on our tender skin.

The others retreated to the bus, but Marie and I pressed on with Squire and Candy.

At the hilltop, we found a small cemetery. Carefully climbing over the barbed-wire fence, we approached a headstone that told us Ex-Corporal James H. Thompson, NWMP, had died in 1923 at the age of sixty-eight. Nearby, we saw his wife's grave, and a small bush with purple flowers.

Cursing the mosquitoes, Squire opened the laptop. After entering the password, I watched Squire at work. On the screen, we saw THOMPSON NWMP 19_ _, followed by the compass coordinates. Squire entered 23 into the date, and immediately a new display appeared: MARSHALL RCMP 19_ _ 49° 19' 51", 104° 82' 23".

"Yes!" Hurrying to the fence, Squire climbed over. Unfortunately, a barb caught his shirt sleeve, ripping it. Squire stamped his foot, cursing loudly. He hurried down the hill, slapping at mosquitoes.

"Gobble, gobble," I said to his retreating back, rolling my eyes. "What a turkey."

Laughing together, we walked down the hill. "Listen," Candy said, "what's going on? Why the laptop and the fancy codes? Why's Squire so anxious to keep moving? What's he after?"

"Sorry," I replied, "but I'm not supposed to say."

"Fair enough," Candy said. "I don't care what happens, as long as I get paid for cooking. As they say, just show me the money!"

Marie smiled at her. "Maybe this will start a new career for you, Candy. You could be a chef at some fancy place like the Temple Gardens resort."

"That's a nice thought."

When we reached the *Mañana Banana*, Marie sighed. "We get to Willow Bunch tonight, Liz. We'll be saying goodbye."

"I know. It's rotten."

Inside the bus, I sat beside Squire. He was studying the SaskMap on his laptop screen. "The search is taking us towards the Big Muddy badlands. The major town in that area is called Coronach—we'd better get more supplies there." Squire looked disapprovingly at Marie. "First, though, we suffer a detour to Willow Bunch. That's a real waste of time."

"Skip Willow Bunch! I'll go with you guys to Coronach."

Aunt Melody shook her head. "Not a chance, Marie. I promised your granny."

"Okay," she said glumly.

Our bus climbed slowly out of the valley. We left the trees and rolling hills behind, and entered an ocean of green stretching in every direction to the horizon.

"This is beautiful," Candy said admiringly. "What a country!"

"Grasslands National Park is nearby," Smollett told her. "I've been there before. I saw deer and antelope, just like in the famous song."

"'Home on the Range,'" Arrow said. "That's a classic."

I studied the SaskMap. "Montana's just south of here. We're really close to the U.S. border."

Smollett nodded. "The 49th parallel—the world's longest undefended boundary."

Shortly after, our path was blocked by white-faced cattle. Approaching them cautiously, Arrow slowed the *Mañana Banana* to a crawl. Herding the cattle along the highway was a young woman on a horse, accompanied by several kids on bikes.

Squire looked at us. "They're moving the cattle from one field to another."

I glanced at Marie. "Mr. Know-it-all," I whispered.

The kids smiled and waved as Arrow carefully threaded a passage between the bellowing animals. Soon the *Mañana Banana* was heading east. As we passed through the pretty town of Rockglen, Arrow said to Squire, "We'll be in Willow Bunch by nightfall. They've got a campground. We can stay overnight."

"Blast! More time wasted."

Marie grew excited as we approached her home town. "There it is," she exclaimed, as a wide valley appeared and we saw the streets and houses of Willow Bunch below. After descending into the valley, we passed a huge sign on the edge of town that read HOME OF THE GIANT and *CHEZ-NOUS DU GÉANT*. Above the words, a young man wearing an old-fashioned top hat waved a welcome. He was enormous.

"Hey," I said, "a real giant!"

"That's Edouard Beaupré. He was born here. His dad was from Quebec and his mom was Métis. Edouard died a long time ago. He was the tallest Canadian of all time."

"How tall was he?"

"Over eight feet—about 250 centimetres."

"Wow. I hope he was a friendly giant."

Marie smiled. "Everyone liked Edouard. He went into a circus, down in the States. Then he died young—it's a sad story." Marie pointed at a three-storey building with a steeple; on the top was a cross. "That's the old convent. Now it's a museum, and they've got things like Edouard's personal ring."

"I wouldn't mind having a look."

Squire shook his head. "No more delays."

10

A sign saying J. L. LEGARE PARK welcomed us to the local campground. I got permission from Aunt Melody to walk into town with Marie. It was a beautiful evening, but I was glum. I didn't want to say goodbye to my friend, especially with her mom still missing.

In town, we stopped at the school grounds to watch kids playing softball, then headed for Marie's home. The streets of the pleasant community were wide and the houses were well kept. Dominating Willow Bunch were several tall grain elevators.

"My brother would be shadowing those elevators," I told Marie, "watching for secret signals between spies."

"Spies and secret signals would never happen in a quiet town like this."

"Maybe not, but so far I've found Saskatchewan a *very* exciting place!"

Outside the Hills of Home Seniors' Club, two men waved a greeting, and a kid waved hello as he rolled past on his skateboard. "Hi, Marie," he said. "How're you doing?"

"What a friendly place," I commented.

"Yeah," Marie said. "Willow Bunch is the best."

"I like the cross, up on that hill."

"At night, the cross is lit with white bulbs. You can see it from all over."

The wind rustled the leaves of a big tree outside Marie's house. The windows were trimmed in green, and the lawn was fringed by flowers. "That's my room," Marie said, pointing up at a window under the peaked roof. "My stepbrother's room is beside mine—he's older than me. Right now, James is boarding with our relatives in Calgary, while he takes a special high school computer course. He's hoping to work for the Gabriel Dumont Institute of Métis Studies."

We went inside. The kitchen was brightly painted in red and white, and had many colourful cookie tins and spice containers. In a corner, big wicker baskets brimmed with onions and potatoes. "Granny's a great cook," Marie said. "So's Mom."

She went into the living room. "Granny, I'm home," she called, but there was no reply. Her face puzzled, Marie walked quickly to a nearby bedroom. "Granny? Where are you?"

I looked into the kitchen. "There's a note beside the phone."

Marie picked it up. "Granny's gone to Coronach. A friend of hers is sick. She says to phone."

As Marie dialed, I wandered into the living room to examine a collection of family photographs. Then Marie appeared beside me. "Here's my dad," she said, pointing at a young man on horseback. He was smiling happily at the camera, framed by pines and blue mountains. "Dad worked at Banff, guiding people on trail rides. Mom says I'm just like him—crazy about horses."

"It's sad that he died."

"Yeah," Marie sighed. Then she cheered up. "Guess what, Liz? Granny was pleased when I said the *Banana* is heading for Coronach. She wonders if I could join her there."

"Hey, we could give you a lift!"

"That's what Granny hopes."

"Great news—but what about school?"

"It's the end of the year—we're not doing much. This way, Granny can stay longer with her friend at Coronach." Marie headed for the stairs. "I'll collect some stuff, then let's tell Squire the good news."

In her bedroom, Marie had large collections of Smurfs and trolls and dolls and ceramic clowns. On the wall was a braided strand of sweetgrass; a poster said *A hug would make my day*. In the window was a dream catcher made with beautiful feathers.

"Mom gave me that," Marie said. "We believe that dreams are messages from the spirit world. When you're sleeping, the dream catcher lets the good ones through, and keeps nightmares from reaching you."

"Cool—I could use a dream catcher myself." I looked into her stepbrother's room. The walls displayed posters of baseball heroes and hot cars, plus an excellent drawing of a wolf. "James did that," Marie said proudly. "Granny says he's a true artist."

"You're not bad either, Marie. Your drawing of Tarantula is excellent."

"Thanks!"

"James is really into computers, eh?"

Marie nodded. "Technology is his first love. That's why he's taking the course in Calgary." She picked up a scanner from a gadget-littered table. "I gave this to James last Christmas. It's for intercepting calls between cell phones."

"Can we try it?"

"Unfortunately, nobody in town has a cell phone." Marie smiled. "My gift was a flop."

"Let's try the scanner in Coronach. Maybe it'll work there."

"Okay! That might be fun."

As we walked through town, a church bell rang somewhere. Evening had arrived, painting the western sky in vivid colours. Warm air brushed our faces.

We stopped to study the museum—the grounds were filled with beautiful lilac bushes. It was a three-storey wooden structure, much like a building one might see in Quebec. "The Sisters of the Cross built this convent in 1914," Marie told me. "Now, as I told you, it's a museum. I could show you a portrait of my ancestors in there, but the museum closes at five o'clock."

"I can see lights in the basement."

"The community centre is down there. People come by until late, so the building is left open."

"Hey, I like those giant footprints painted on the sidewalk."

"They are supposed to be Edouard's. He took a size 22. See the statue of Edouard outside the museum? That's where his grave is."

"Let's go have a look."

The air was sweet with the smell of lilacs as we followed the footprints to the giant's grave. Above it rose the statue of the young man, arm raised in greeting. He was very, very tall.

Marie looked up at the giant's face. "Edouard dreamed of being a cowboy in the Big Muddy badlands. He could ride and lasso with the best, but had to give up when his legs got so long they touched the ground when he was on horseback."

"Wow—that's tall!"

"Edouard joined a circus freak show to get money for his family. I bet he was homesick, but he never came back to Willow Bunch. He died of tuberculosis at the age of twenty-three while appearing at the St. Louis World's Fair. And guess what, Liz? He didn't get buried for eighty-six years."

"How come?"

"Edouard's family had no money to bring him home. So instead, his body was exhibited in store windows in St. Louis."

"Gross and disgusting!"

"After that, an eastern university got control of Edouard's mummified body. His nephew had to fight the university for fifteen years to get a decent burial for Edouard."

I shook my head. "That's totally uncivilized."

Back at the campground, Marie's return got the response we'd expected from Squire. "Another mouth to feed!" he complained.

Smollett looked up from the campfire, where he was spooning baked beans from a blackened pot. "It's my money, Squire. I admire Marie's determination to find her mother. I welcome her return."

"Thanks," Marie said quietly, giving Smollett a grateful look.

"No problem, young lady. Now, have some of Candy's lip-smacking Boston baked beans. They are as fabulous as Candy herself."

We helped ourselves to beans and took them to a wooden picnic table. The others sat by the fire, staring at the flames as they munched Candy's delicious meal.

Arrow looked at the sky. It was vast, and black, and tossed with a multitude of stars. "What's out there?" he said. "I need to know!"

"I don't," Candy replied. "All I need is peace and quiet. I'm so happy this evening."

When we'd finished eating, Marie went to sit beside Arrow. They spoke quietly for several minutes, then Arrow shook his head. Looking unhappy, Marie returned to my side. "Arrow won't help me find Mom. I wanted to drive to Assiniboia tonight in the *Banana*. It's not too far, and maybe we'd spot her."

"But he wouldn't do it? That's too bad."

Marie kicked at the dirt. "I think Arrow's falling for Candy. She's got him convinced that Mom ran away with those bikers. He's totally lost faith in Mom. That's why he won't help me find her."

"Candy wants Arrow a lot, eh? It's almost pathetic."

"Love." Marie shook her head. "Go figure."

Smollett stood up beside the campfire. "Candy, your cooking is wonderful." He looked at Squire. "Let's have a meeting."

Squire scowled. "If you insist."

Walking away a short distance, the men fell into a heated discussion. Their words didn't reach us, but I saw anger on their faces. "Those guys and their meetings," I said. "What's going on?"

Squire bellowed something, then tried to shove Smollett. But he was quick on his feet, and easily avoided Squire's attack. Putting a thumb against his nose, Smollett wiggled his fingers at Squire while making rude noises.

Aunt Melody laughed. "Those two guys! What a circus they are."

I looked at her. "Okay to go for a walk with Marie?"

"Sure, but don't go far."

"Just along the path to the hillside where they've got that big cross. Want to come with us, Aunt Melody?"

She shook her head. "Thanks, but I've got studying to do."

* * *

Reaching the cross, we looked down at the streets of Willow Bunch. Lights shone from the houses. Not one person moved through the quiet streets. Above our heads, the cross glowed against the night sky. "A farmer owns this land," Marie said. "The lightbulbs are connected to his power supply." She took out the scanner. "Let's try this, okay? Maybe someone's finally got a cell phone."

We listened to noises and squeals from a small speaker. Then a man's voice suddenly emerged: "*Advise your position. Over.*"

The scanner fell silent. "We're only getting half the conversation," Marie said. "I could search for the other half, but I'm not sure how."

"Let's stay with this guy."

After a moment, more came from the scanner: "*An abandoned church. We've got problems here—I need twenty-four hours extra. It's urgent you arrange it. Over and out.*"

We listened a while, but heard nothing more. Deciding to call it a night, we started back along the hilltop, discussing the message we'd heard on the scanner. A magnificent moon had risen, spreading its silver radiance over the land. It shadowed distant hills, and glowed on the grass surrounding us.

I didn't think I was tired, but I entered dreamland the moment my head hit the pillow. When I opened my eyes in the morning, I saw Marie's face. "Hey, Liz, guess what? The bus won't start."

Squire's face was beet red as he watched Arrow poking around under the hood. You could almost see smoke coming out of his ears. "The bus was fixed just *yesterday*," he bellowed. "How can it be dead again?"

Arrow wiped his hands on an oily rag. "I can't tell you, boss. I'll have to walk to the gas station in town and get help from an expert. I think it's the same problem we had at Gravelbourg."

Stamping his feet in a dance of frustration, Squire marched up and down beside the ashes of the campfire. "Blast it— *another* delay! What is this, a conspiracy?"

* * *

We'd just finished a late lunch when a tow truck finally arrived to collect the *Mañana Banana*. We walked into Willow Bunch behind the bus, saw it deposited at the gas station, and then wandered around town.

At the museum, Aunt Melody took a picture of the statue of the giant. Inside the old convent, the cool air was pleasant after the heat outside. We were asked to sign the guest register by our guide, a university student named Jordan. He had blond hair and a friendly manner.

I looked at Edouard's enormous ring in a display case. "How does a person grow to be so huge?"

Jordan aimed his blue eyes at me. My heart went pitty-pat. "His gland—"

"A giant's pituitary gland malfunctions," Squire interrupted. "It produces too much growth hormone."

Jordan looked at him. "That's correct, sir."

"I know about these things, lad."

I leaned close to Marie's ear. "I *hate* Squire."

Jordan showed us the giant's baptismal certificate. "Edouard was a shy and gentle man. When kids teased him, he'd lift them onto a roof until they apologized. Edouard was incredibly powerful—he could raise a horse on his shoulders."

Squire yawned. "History bores me."

Jordan ignored him. "Twenty kids were born in Edouard's family," he told us. "But many infants died back then, so only eight survived into childhood."

As we followed Jordan into a hallway, I said, "I *really* like this museum!"

"Thank you," he said happily.

The hallway was lined with wooden doors. "In this convent," Jordan said, "the Sisters of the Cross established a school for kids from distant farms. Saskatchewan winters are harsh. Staying here, the kids never missed a day of classes because of the weather."

"Those poor kids," I joked, and was rewarded with a laugh from Jordan.

The hallway was filled with local history. We studied photographs of the giant and his family, then the uniform of the Willow Bunch Giants baseball team, and the personal rocking chair of a woman who had weighed 425 pounds.

Marie pulled me over to a photograph. A pioneer family stared at us with solemn faces. "My ancestors," she said proudly. Then we studied an enormous shoe displayed on a wooden stand. "This was made by a store in Moose Jaw," Jordan explained. "The shoe's supposed to be a replica of Edouard's, but it's only a size 16."

"He took a size 22," I said. "Right?"

Jordan looked at me with surprise. "Excellent!"

As we followed Jordan upstairs, Marie grinned at me. "I told you that size," she whispered.

"Yes, and I'm eternally grateful!"

In the upper hallway, we were greeted by a life-sized mannequin of a bride in a white gown. There were lots of old photos on the walls, plus huge wooden masks made by a local resident.

One room contained the giant's enormous bed. Edouard himself stood in a corner, cane in hand. "That papier-mâché replica was made in 1970 to celebrate the Centennial of Willow Bunch." Jordan looked up at the giant's unhappy eyes. "Edouard was an intelligent man. He spoke four languages, including Cree and Sioux. He might have found a cure for cancer, but instead was fated to become a circus freak."

In another room was a poster that advertised a long-ago gig at the local theatre by Furzee the Magician. *See! Him Cut off a Human Head Before Your Very Eyes,* the poster proclaimed, and then, *See Him Carry a Head into the Audience and give it away.*

"Who got the body?" I asked, feeling pleased when both Arrow and Jordan chuckled.

Candy studied a wall of licence plates dating as far back as 1926, then examined a soldier's helmet from the First World War. I tried on a beekeeper's helmet but didn't like it; the thick veil over my face made me feel claustrophobic. "It would make a good disguise," I said.

As Smollett tried it on, I examined a prison cell in the corner. Going inside, I sat on the uncomfortable iron bed.

"This prison cell belonged to the local Mounties," Jordan said to me through the bars. "When the Willow Bunch detachment was closed, the RCMP donated the cell to our museum." Suddenly, he slammed the door shut, and slapped a big padlock on it. "Now you're my prisoner."

"Hey," I yelped. "Let me out!"

Laughing, Jordan opened the padlock with a key from the wall. "I'm just teasing. Sorry, Liz."

"How'd you know my name?"

"You wrote it in the guest book."

I glanced at Marie, feeling mighty pleased. Then something unfortunate happened: as we went downstairs, a woman passed us, heading up. "It's bad luck to pass on the stairs," I whispered to Marie. "*Very* bad luck."

Sure enough, when we reached the lobby, a pretty girl was waiting with a kiss and a hug for Jordan. "His girlfriend," Marie told me. "They broke up, but I guess they're back together again."

As we left the museum, I waved a sad farewell to Jordan. "Dreams die hard," I commented bitterly.

"Isn't Jordan a bit old for you?"

"Maybe. But I still feel sorry for myself."

At the gas station, the hood was up on the *Mañana Banana*. "A few more hours," the mechanic reported, "and you'll be mobile. I'm waiting for a part to arrive from Assiniboia."

Squire groaned. "I don't believe it. We've lost another full day."

"Don't worry about it," Smollett said. "I noticed the local motel has a restaurant—let's have supper." He turned to Candy. "I hope you'll join us."

"I guess so, if you're buying."

I looked at Marie. "A full day lost. On the cell phone, that guy requested a delay of twenty-four hours. I wonder if there's a connection?"

Smollett glanced suddenly at me. As he did, Arrow looked at the mechanic. "What happened to my bus?"

"Sabotage."

"*What*?"

"This damage was deliberately done. You folks got any enemies?"

"Of course not," Arrow exclaimed.

"It's just a run of bad luck," Smollett said smoothly. "Come on, folks, let's go eat something. The treat's on me."

Outside the garage, Aunt Melody looked at me. "Sabotage! This is getting serious. It's time to go home."

"Aunt Melody, no! That would be terrible."

Squire nodded his agreement. "We've come so far, Melody. We're sure to be as rich as kings!" He looked at me with hopeful eyes. "Of course, if Liz would only tell me the password . . . "

"Not a chance," I declared.

Squire turned back to Aunt Melody. "I'm sure there'll be no trouble."

"Are you still in touch with the police, Squire?"

"Of course!"

Smollett looked at Aunt Melody. "We'll make sure nothing goes wrong. Just trust us, Melody."

"Well, okay." She looked at her watch. "I'm walking back to the campground. I've got some serious studying to do. Liz and Marie, don't be late."

"Sure thing, Aunt Melody." I said goodbye to her, then walked with the others to the Stagecoach, a combination motel and restaurant. Several dusty pickup trucks were parked in the lot; inside, people sat at wooden booths and tables. As we entered, they all stared.

"Come meet my friends," Marie said, taking me to a table where two kids were drinking milkshakes. "Liz, these are my buddies, Aaron Spink and Jenna Bennett." They were very friendly, and we had fun talking.

Then Marie and I joined the others; Smollett was looking at a newspaper. On page one, a headline screamed "Superstar doubles reward again!" The picture showed Winter Leigh surrounded by reporters and TV cameras.

Squire drank some water. "The reward has increased in value, yet again." He glanced at Smollett. "Does this change your opinion?"

Smollett shook his head. "Not in the slightest."

I studied the picture of Winter Leigh. "The pressure is getting to her. She's looking tense."

"The golden statue is very special to Winter Leigh," Squire told me. "It was a gift from her husband. Before his death, he was a famous and wealthy movie producer. He discovered Winter Leigh, and made her a star."

"You know a lot about her," Candy commented.

Squire shrugged his big shoulders. "I've been a fan of Winter Leigh for many years. I've seen every movie she's made, and read all the books about her. I'm a frequent visitor to her website. That golden statue has a special place in Winter Leigh's heart. If I ever found it, I'd be sure it was returned to her."

"But you'd accept the reward," Smollett said.

"Of course! It's a substantial amount of money."

Smollett paid the bill, and the adults left the restaurant. As Marie and I talked to Jenna and Aaron, Marie suddenly stood up. "I'm going home for the sweet-grass—I want it with me on the trip, just for luck. I'm also phoning Granny, so you might as well stay here, Liz. I won't be too long."

Eventually, I went outside to wait for Marie. Night had fallen. On the hill, the white lights of the cross glowed against the dark sky. The air was deliciously warm and the moon was beautiful.

I could see Arrow inside the gas station, but the others had disappeared. Somewhere in the night, a coyote howled with a lonesome sound. Wondering what was keeping Marie, I wandered across the parking lot to West Street and stood looking at the nearby museum. The windows were dark; the grounds were shadowed by shrubs and trees.

Suddenly, a light flashed from an upstairs window.

I blinked my eyes, thinking I was mistaken. But it came again, from the same museum window: *dash—dot—dot—* "It's Morse code," I whispered to myself. "Someone's signalling with a flashlight."

Thankful I'd studied the code in Guides, I grabbed a stick and scratched letters in the dirt as the light flashed:

C...O...R...O...N...A...C...H

"Coronach! That's where we're going next!"

The signals stopped. Quickly, I ran back to the restaurant to leave a message with Jenna and Aaron. "Please tell Marie I've gone to the museum," I said. Back outside, I hurried along West Street, and followed the giant footprints to the front door of the museum. It was unlocked.

142

"I'll be fine," I whispered to myself, then touched the wooden door for luck.

Taking a deep breath, I stepped inside.

11

The museum was dark and silent. Moonlight gleamed through windows, showing the stairs to the upper hallway.

I started towards them, moving cautiously. Then my toe hit something, and I stumbled. Blundering for support, I knocked over the display of the giant's shoe. *Crash*! The sound echoed in my ears over and over.

Quickly, I ran up the stairs, hoping I'd find a light switch at the top. But, instead, a woman was waiting, one hand raised. I gasped in shock, then realized it was the bride mannequin.

My heart beat hard as I looked at the giant, standing alone in the gloom. Across the hallway was the room where someone had been signalling. Slowly, I stepped inside—no one stood at the window, and no sound was heard. In a shadowed corner was the prison cell, dark and ominous.

I glanced at the display of helmets on the wall—the beekeeper's was missing. As my brain registered this disturbing information, something moved in the prison cell.

I cried out, horrified. Inside the cell, the shadows changed shape. A person rose out of the darkness, face hidden inside the beekeeper's helmet, and grabbed me. As I screamed, I was dragged into the cell and tripped, falling heavily to the floor.

The door slammed shut. "No," I cried, as the padlock was slapped into place and locked. "Don't—please don't!"

Moments later, the person was gone. I was alone.

* * *

Soon after, I heard footsteps. Slow and cautious, they were coming my way. Huddling back inside the iron cage, I tried to see through the darkness.

A shape appeared in the doorway. "Liz?" a voice whispered.

"Marie! Is it really you?"

She hurried forward. "Are you okay, Liz?"

"Yes, but I'm *so* happy to see you!"

"The key's on the wall—I'll get it." She looked around nervously. "Then let's get out of this dark place. It gives me the creeps."

Moments later, Marie had the door unlocked, and we hugged. "I talked to Granny a long time," Marie explained. "That's what delayed me. When I returned to the Stagecoach, Aaron and Jenna told me you were here. Coming down the street, I saw someone run out the door."

"Who was it? Could you see?"

Marie shook her head. "Not with that beekeeper's helmet." She shivered. "I came into the museum. It was so dark and scary, I didn't think I could do it. But I kept going."

"We mustn't mention this to anyone. *Especially* Aunt Melody."

Marie nodded. "I understand."

*   *   *

We reached Coronach in the early morning. Arrow stopped the bus at the tourist bureau, and we got out to stretch our legs. As Candy lit up, Aunt Melody looked disapproving. "I watched a friend die of lung cancer in a hospital bed. It was a slow and painful death."

"I'm sorry for your friend, Melody, but I was born lucky." Candy blew grey smoke into the clean, sweet air. "Cigarettes won't kill me."

Marie looked at a mural of local history on the tourist bureau's wall. "Coronach was a beautiful race-horse," she said, studying the noble head of the British champion that gave the town its name. "Granny's friend has horses. We could go riding."

"Hey, that would be great!"

Squire glanced impatiently our way. "There'll be no riding if it delays this expedition."

Back on the bus, we drove south on the town's main

street, past shops and restaurants and the office for Coronach and District Tours. As in other towns we'd travelled through, the tallest structure was the water tower.

Heading for a farm on the outskirts of Coronach, we followed a gravel road past fields of green. Then we turned into a long driveway leading to the farm. "There's Granny," Marie exclaimed, as two women came outside waving a welcome.

Marie gave her grandmother a big hug, then introduced us. Her grandmother's name was Claire; I liked her pleasant eyes and good-natured smile. Her friend, Lily, was also very nice. "I'm feeling much better since Claire came to visit," Lily said. "Come inside. The coffee's on and we've got delicious lemonade for the girls."

"Not a chance," Squire replied. "We're in a hurry. There's no time for socializing."

"I'm staying for a visit," Aunt Melody told him, "and so is Liz. Marie has invited her to go horseback riding. Do some shopping in town, Cousin, then pick us up later."

"Really, Melody, I must protest."

Smollett shook his head. "Never argue with a woman, Squire. Let's go into town for a coffee. It'll give me a chance to call my office for messages."

"Very well, if you insist." Squire looked at Candy. "Are you coming with us?"

"I might as well. I can get supplies—we're running low on a few things."

Marie and I hurried to the stables, where I approached the horses nervously—they seemed huge. But mine was a gentle creature named Buddy, and we got along nicely. Within a short time, I'd learned the basics of riding from Marie, and was ready to explore the countryside.

But first we went into the house to tell them where we were going. "Aunt Melody," I said, "we're off for our ride."

Claire looked at Marie. "Where are you going?"

"Paisley Brook School. We won't be long."

"Have fun, then, but be careful."

Aunt Melody turned to me. "Don't take chances."

"No problem, Aunt Melody." I put my backpack on the kitchen floor. "I'll leave this here for safekeeping."

"I'm taking my sash," Marie said. "It might come in handy on the ride."

Outside, she put the sash in a saddlebag. "Paisley Brook is an abandoned one-room school," she explained. "It's in the middle of nowhere. There are old wooden desks, and ancient maps on the wall. You can see countries that don't even exist now."

"The Husbands—the people who run Benbow Farm— attended a school like that. George said there was only one teacher for all the grades. Amazing, eh?"

Buddy plodded comfortably along a prairie trail behind Marie and her chestnut mare, Sundance. We weren't the only ones enjoying the gorgeous day—grasshoppers whirred through the hot air, and gophers sunned themselves outside their tunnel entrances. Seeing us approach, they whistled warnings to each other, then escaped into their underground world.

I sniffed the air; it was filled with tantalizing scents. "The wildflowers are so beautiful," I called to Marie.

"You know what? I still think we'll find the Sacred Egyptian Cat."

"That would be so cool!"

"It's fun sharing my theories with you, Marie. I couldn't get Aunt Melody very interested—she's too busy studying." I turned my face to the sun. "Anyway, I'm keeping a close eye on Squire. Aunt Melody deserves some of the reward, but he may cheat her."

"He'd better not," Marie replied indignantly. Then she pointed at a low hill. "The school's on the other side."

"You seem to know this country well."

She nodded. "I've stayed at Lily's farm lots of times. I've explored all over on horseback."

At the top of the hill, we looked down at the deserted schoolhouse. A flagless flagpole stood beside the small building, and there was a big shed nearby. The empty schoolyard seemed a lonely place.

Marie turned to me. "See the dirt behind the shed? Aren't those tire tracks?"

I squinted my eyes. "You're right."

"They could be from motorcycles!"

I glanced at Marie. "Want to take a closer look?"

"Yes. Mom could be down there." She got out her colourful sash. "Maybe we can use this."

After tethering the horses, we scurried down the hill to the shed. "These tracks are recent," Marie whispered, examining the dirt.

I looked in a cracked window. "There's a motorcycle inside—it's got a California plate!"

"Let's get closer."

Peering around the shed, we studied the abandoned

building. Nothing moved behind the windows. "One," I whispered, "two, three . . . "

Leaping from hiding, we dashed across the yard to shelter against the wall of the schoolhouse. Heart thundering, I peeked in the window at a blackboard and a large map of Africa on the wall. There was no sign of anyone.

"Let's check the cellar."

An outside door hung on its hinges; the ceiling inside was high. In the gloom, I saw a jumble of old lumber and piles of musty textbooks. There was a door in a back corner. Faded lettering said MEDICAL ROOM. Nearby, stairs led to the floor above.

We heard snoring from inside the medical room. Cautiously, I tried the door—it wouldn't open. We tiptoed along the wall, looking for another way into the room. Then I spotted a heating grate. Dropping to our knees, we peered through. Dim light filtered into the room through a dirty window.

Inside the room, Tarantula sprawled on a chair, snoring loudly. Beside him was a big table, scattered with lots of beer cans. Nearby were a couple of metal cots with thin mattresses; handcuffed to the cots were two women.

One was Sister Rita, and the other was Teresa.

* * *

For a long moment, Marie stared at her mother. Then, slowly, she worked the grate loose. The hole it left in the wall was too small for me, but not for Marie. "I'm going in there," she whispered.

"Be careful!"

"Don't worry—that guy's out like a light."

Marie crawled through the opening and cautiously approached her mother. Heart in my throat, I watched Tarantula, praying he'd stay asleep. Marie shook her mother awake; Teresa was startled, but didn't make a sound. When Marie whispered a question, her mom pointed at the table.

On it was a key. Marie opened her mother's handcuffs, then she released Sister Rita. Meanwhile, the biker snored on, unaware that Marie had released his hostages and was now—slowly and carefully—handcuffing him to one of the metal cots.

Unlocking the door, Marie led her mother and Sister Rita out of the room. We crept out of the cellar and seconds later we were all in the sunshine, hurrying across the schoolyard towards safety. Sister Rita moved slowly, but Marie's mother gave her support and before long we'd climbed the hill to the horses.

At long last, Marie could speak. "Mom," she cried, throwing her arms around her mother. "Mom, I love you."

I turned to Sister Rita. "Are you okay?"

She nodded, smiling happily. "I prayed all the time, and God sent help. When you girls came to the cathedral, I tried to make you leave. Those motorcycle people were hiding in the bishop's house. I was afraid you'd be captured, too."

I looked at Marie's mother. "Why were you taken hostage?"

"I don't know," Teresa replied, "but thanks for the rescue!"

"Where are the rest of the bikers?"

"There was a big argument last night. The others took off. They said they were going back to California. Tarantula was really angry. He's been drinking heavily, ever since they left."

"Let's ride into town fast," I said. "The police have to get here before Tarantula wakes up and escapes."

Marie's mother turned to Sister Rita. "You ride with me, Sister. The girls can take the other horse."

*   *   *

After a long ride in the hot sunshine, we arrived at the farm. Lily, Claire, and Aunt Melody stared in astonishment at Sister Rita and Teresa as they entered the kitchen on shaky legs.

Quickly, we told our story; when it ended, Aunt Melody gave me a big smile. "Liz, you really do have detective skills. Congratulations—I'm so proud of you girls!" Then she grabbed the phone. "I'm calling the Mounties so they can arrest that biker."

After a long conversation with the RCMP, she hung up the phone. "They're coming, but it'll take a while. Their nearest detachment is a long way from here."

Through the window, I saw the *Mañana Banana* approaching. As we went outside, I glanced at Marie's mom—her brown eyes glowed with happiness, and I realized how much she loved Arrow.

He was astonished to see Teresa. For a moment, he just stared, then a huge grin creased his handsome face. "Teresa! I've missed you so much."

As they kissed, I looked at Candy. She watched

their happiness with a tiny smile on her face. "Teresa's lucky," she said wistfully.

"You'll find a nice guy, Candy. Wait and see."

"Thanks, Liz. I hope so."

After Teresa told Arrow about being a hostage, he offered his hand to Marie. "You were right, believing in your mom. She never deserted me. I apologize."

Marie smiled. "It's a happy ending, Arrow. That's what counts."

Candy turned to me. "What exactly happened, Liz? Where'd you find Teresa and Sister Rita?"

I described the events at Paisley Brook School. "Tarantula is asleep, just waiting to be captured!"

"I'm going out there," Arrow said. "I want to make sure he's securely handcuffed."

Candy was astonished. "That sounds dangerous!"

"Maybe," Arrow replied, "but those creeps took Teresa hostage. I want revenge."

Squire's face was beet red. "But our expedition, man!"

"It will have to wait."

"Blast!" Squire marched up and down in fury, then turned to Arrow. "Very well, but I'm going with you. The moment the Mounties have arrived, we'll continue our search."

Arrow nodded. "Agreed."

"I'll go, too," Teresa said to Arrow.

"Not a chance," he replied. "You've been through a terrible experience, Teresa. You need a medical checkup, then some rest."

"Please, can't you stay here, honey?"

"If only! We're being paid for the expedition,

Teresa. I've *got* to drive these people, or no money."

"Okay," she said reluctantly. "But I've missed you so much."

Marie smiled at her. "I'll stay with you, Mom."

"That would be really nice, honey." Teresa looked at Arrow. "Come back safely."

Smollett headed for the bus. "Let's get moving."

"I'm staying here," Aunt Melody declared. "Sister Rita and Teresa have been through a terrible experience. They need help and support." She looked at me. "You'd better stay here, Liz."

"But *why?* There's no danger—Tarantula is in handcuffs."

"Still . . ."

Squire looked at her. "Please, Melody, let Liz go with us. Without the password, our expedition can't continue."

Smollett nodded. "I've spent a lot of money."

"I'll keep an eye on Liz," Candy offered. "I enjoy her company. She'll be fine."

"Very well, I agree."

"Thanks, Candy," I exclaimed. "Thanks, Aunt Melody!"

Marie handed me a key. "This unlocks the handcuffs. It fits both pairs."

"Thanks," I said, slipping the key into my backpack.

"Take care," Marie said. "Safe journey."

I smiled at her. "You sound anxious, but I'll be fine."

"I hope so." She handed me her sweetgrass. "This helped me find Mom. Now it may help you, too."

"Thank you so much, Marie. I'll see you soon."

154

*   *   *

Lily provided directions by road to the school. On the bus, I put my backpack in a corner. As we got underway, Candy looked at Squire. "Cheer up, guy. You're a total brain with that computer. I'm sure you'll find whatever you're searching for." She studied his face, then shook her head. "But maybe it won't bring you happiness."

"And maybe it will," Squire growled.

Eventually, we arrived at the schoolhouse. Arrow got a flashlight from the bus, then went inside. Long minutes passed while we watched the schoolhouse. I shuffled from foot to foot; Arrow seemed to be taking a long time.

Then he appeared. "There's a biker in the cellar, handcuffed to a cot. He's not a happy camper."

We hurried into the school, anxious to see the captive. In the cellar we crowded into the medical room, where Tarantula sat in handcuffs. His eyes raged with anger. I held back nervously, and so did Candy.

"Where's the key for those handcuffs?" Squire asked me. "The police will need to release him."

"In my pack," I said. "It's on the *Banana*."

Squire turned to Arrow. "Any duct tape on the bus?"

"Sure thing."

"Good. We'll leave the key taped to the front door. The Mounties can release this guy when they arrest him, and meanwhile we can continue our expedition. We've done our duty, making sure this biker's still a captive."

"Fair enough," Arrow said.

Leaving Tarantula alone in the medical room, we went outside. The heat was intense, making me sweat. "I don't like this weather," Arrow said, studying the sky. "Something's going to happen."

Squire looked at me. "You get the key, Liz. Arrow, find the duct tape."

Inside the bus, I picked up my pack. As I did, I heard the sound of thunder. I looked towards the shed—the noise had come from there. Then, as we all gazed in astonishment, a huge motorcycle wheeled into the yard. On it was Tarantula, no longer our prisoner.

12

The biker roared across the yard. Spinning to a stop at the road, he threw a look of hatred in our direction. Then he gunned his engine and took off fast.

"How'd he get free?" Squire demanded.

Quickly, I rummaged through my pack. "The handcuff key is gone!" I dashed madly to the schoolhouse, followed by the others. In the cellar, I ran to the medical room, where the handcuffs lay on the floor. There was no sign of the key.

"Maybe he picked the lock," Candy suggested.

Smollett looked at me. "Got any holes in your pockets?"

"Why?"

"That's where you probably put the key. It fell on the floor and the biker grabbed it."

"No way," I protested. "The key was in my pack."

"Who cares?" Squire looked at his watch. "Let's get moving. That biker's gone, and there's nothing we can do. We've got to reach the compass coordinates before nightfall."

"What about that guy Tarantula?" Candy asked in a trembling voice.

Squire dismissed her fears with a wave. "He'll have crossed the border by now."

"Maybe we should wait for the Mounties," Arrow suggested.

Squire shook his head. "We'll report to them tomorrow. That biker has escaped, but the hostages are safe. A pretty good outcome, I'd say, so let's get moving."

Candy looked at Squire. "A good outcome?" She shivered. "I don't agree."

*   *   *

We climbed into the bus. I was worried about the key— I'd have sworn it was in my pack. As the *Mañana Banana* got underway, I watched the horizon for motorcycles, but saw only hawks on the wing and a sleek antelope sprinting across a green field. Daredevil gophers darted across the dusty road before our bus, cheered on by their friends, but I didn't enjoy their antics. I was too busy worrying; somehow, I sensed that Tarantula still lurked close by.

The land changed, becoming more rugged. We entered a valley sheltered between soaring sandstone cliffs. "These badlands have existed a long time," Smollett told me. "A glacier carved out this valley."

"It reminds me of cowboy movies. Why's this place called Big Muddy?"

"Not far from here is a big, muddy lake. These badlands once crawled with crooks and rustlers and horse thieves. But after the Mounties arrived, things settled down."

In the distance, alone at the centre of the valley, was a hill with steep sides. "That landform is called a butte," Smollett explained. "It's a relic of the Ice Age."

Arrow glanced at me in the mirror. "This is sacred country to Native peoples. Near Big Beaver, there's a buffalo effigy. We still gather there on important occasions."

"What's an effigy?" I asked.

"It represents the spirit of the animal. Long ago, rocks were laid out in the shape of a buffalo. They've never been touched since then. For centuries, my people have gathered at the effigy."

Arrow looked at the lonely hill. "From up on top, scouts would watch for herds of buffalo or an approaching enemy."

"Hey, I see caves! I'd love to explore them."

"Not a chance," barked Squire. "We're pressing on. Is that understood?"

Arrow turned the wheel sharply. The bus swerved onto a dirt road and bumped its way towards the hill. Squire shouted a protest, but Arrow ignored him. When the bus stopped, he turned to Squire.

"I'm sick of you, mister. You give all the orders, and Smollett pays the bills. You're a waste of time." He opened the door. "Liz wants to explore, and she's getting the chance."

Seizing the moment, I darted off the bus. "I'll be back soon," I called. "Thanks, Arrow!"

As I hurried away, Squire got off the bus. "Come back here," he bellowed at me. "I demand that we leave immediately!"

Ignoring him, I began to climb the steep slope. Centuries of savage weather had carved deep fissures into the sandstone; my feet slipped and slid, but I made progress. Above, I could see the gaping black mouths of caves where pigeons flew in and out, cooing in the hot air.

I entered a cave; it was cool inside. I was surrounded by hardened grey dirt extending about 10 metres into the heart of the sandstone. Feeling a bit claustrophobic, I quickly explored and then returned to sunshine.

Looking down, I was surprised at how high I'd climbed. Far below, the *Mañana Banana* was a vivid yellow against the wild grass. A tiny Candy waved to me. "Be careful, Liz," her miniature voice called. "It's dangerous."

Waving a reassuring signal to Candy, I continued my climb. At the top, the view was magnificent. Pretending to be a Native warrior, I studied the valley and distant cliffs for signs of trouble. It was fun, but I missed Marie.

I looked down. To my surprise, Squire was climbing the slope with Smollett. Reaching a cave, they stopped to talk. I couldn't hear anything, but both seemed very upset. Squire shouted something and shoved Smollett. Staggering backwards, Smollett somehow managed to remain standing. Squire lunged again, but Smollett ducked out of the way. Losing his balance, Squire cried out in horror. Then he fell, rolling and tumbling down the slope. As dust rose behind him, he plunged into the wild grass and lay still.

"Oh no," I cried.

Candy and Arrow ran from the bus to kneel over Squire. As Smollett descended the slope to join them, I hurried down with dirt cascading from my feet.

Squire was groaning in pain. "My leg," he moaned. "I think it's broken!"

"Where's the nearest doctor?" Candy asked.

"Coronach," Arrow replied. "We'll take him there in the bus."

"No," Squire cried in horror. "You can't! I'm so close to the treasure, I can't lose it now!"

"Nonsense," Smollett replied. "Your leg's a mess— you must get help."

There was sweat on Squire's face. He stared hard at Smollett. "You win again."

Smollett chuckled gleefully. "Learn to control your temper, Squire. It's a liability."

Poor Squire. He looked so unhappy. But Smollett glowed with pleasure.

"I love defeating you, Squire. I'll be even richer, and your leg will be in a cast. It's really quite funny!"

"I'm not laughing," Squire scowled.

Smollett's eyes went to the road. "I see a pickup truck approaching. Let's ask the driver to take Squire into town. The rest of us can continue on."

Candy looked at me. "Maybe you should go with them, Liz."

"Not a chance!"

"Are you sure? Things could turn dangerous."

I laughed. "You can't scare me, Candy. I want to know what happens next—I'm staying."

Hurrying to the roadside, Smollett flagged down the pickup. The driver was a young guy with a shaved head. He agreed to drive Squire to the doctor, and I asked him to phone Lily as well. "Please tell my aunt I'm okay."

"Sure, no problem."

Squire groaned as the young guy helped him into the pickup. "I've been cheated. I was going to be a rich man."

"Yeah, right," he replied, putting the truck in gear. "And next week I'm winning the lottery."

Arrow looked at Smollett. "Are we continuing the expedition, Mr. Smollett?"

"I hope so." He turned to me. "You've watched Squire use the laptop, right?"

I nodded.

"Would you take over from Squire, and help find the golden statue? We'll all share the reward, of course."

"Sure, I'll help," I said. "But how'd you know we were looking for the statue?"

"It was easy to figure out," Smollett replied, as we climbed into the bus. "By the time we reached Avonlea I'd guessed the truth. That's why I invested money in this expedition." Smollett chuckled. "I've known Squire since high school. I'm lucky—money attaches itself to me. But Squire's the opposite—he does nothing but stumble from crisis to crisis. This time he's really lost out." He turned to Arrow. "Now, let's get moving. I'm certain the Sacred Egyptian Cat is close by."

* * *

After we got underway, I entered the secret password. The SaskMap appeared, tracking our progress across the Big Muddy badlands. We turned off Highway 18 and rolled south on a gravel road. The countryside looked hot and dusty; the skies were dark with threatening clouds.

Beeping sounded from the SaskMap as we approached the coordinates of latitude and longitude that we'd learned at the grave near Wood Mountain. "See the hill ahead?" I said to Arrow. "That's where the laptop's leading us."

I turned to Smollett. "Maybe a Mountie is buried up there. Just like at Wood Mountain."

A dirt road curved up the hillside. Engine straining, our faithful *Mañana Banana* made the climb and stopped at a rocky outcropping. Overlooking the magnificent view was a small cemetery, totally alone in the emerald-coloured world.

"I see an RCMP crest on a tombstone," Smollett said. "Good guess, Liz."

Greatly excited, we hurried to the cemetery. I looked at the Mountie crest, and then at the inscription: *1470, James Marshall, RCMP, 1866-1944.* "What does 1470 mean?"

"That's his RCMP regimental number," Smollett replied.

Arrow looked down the hill. "I can see the remains

of some old building. Maybe it was a Mountie post, and this guy Marshall served here."

"You're probably right," Candy said. "He must have asked to be buried on this beautiful hillside."

I entered 44 into the code; the screen blinked as new coordinates appeared, followed by the words SEC HERE.

"What does *SEC* stand for?" Arrow asked.

I glanced at him. "Sacred Egyptian Cat."

"I knew it," Smollett exclaimed gleefully. "We're about to find the golden statue!"

Quickly, I entered the latest coordinates into the SaskMap. A topographical map of Big Muddy appeared on the screen. Highway 18 was shown in red, and the back roads in yellow. A dotted line marked the 49th parallel. "The coordinates meet close to the border," I said. "I think Billy Bones brought the cat here. He stole it from the Death Machine and they've been trying to find it."

Smollett rushed towards the bus. "Then let's get moving! Those bikers could still be around, searching. We must find the statue first."

*   *   *

The *Mañana Banana* made its careful way down the hill, then turned in the direction of the highway. "At Highway 18, go left," I told Arrow, keeping an eye on the laptop screen.

Candy put a cassette on the stereo, then went into the WC and closed the door as heavy metal blasted from the speakers.

"I hate Candy's choice of music," Smollett muttered. "Other than that, she's the perfect woman."

After washing and drying her hands, Candy dropped the towel into the laundry hamper. She plugged in the kettle for coffee. "I hope Squire's okay. That was a nasty fall."

"Whose idea was the climb?" I asked Smollett.

"Mine. I wanted a meeting in private."

"I saw the accident. I was higher up the hill."

Smollett stared at me. I didn't know what he was thinking. Then he leaned over Arrow at the wheel, gripping his shoulder. "Faster, man, faster."

After Highway 18, we took a gravel road that wandered south towards the border. Sandstone hills surrounded us; above, the sky looked scary—the clouds were deep blue and black, and they'd become an alarming size. They boiled and seethed, looking very angry.

"Should we be worried about the weather?" I asked.

"I don't know," Candy said. "Maybe . . . "

Something beeped inside the bus. I was startled, so were the others. When the beep sounded again, Smollett searched inside the laundry hamper. His hand emerged holding a cell phone. "What's this doing here?" Smollett said, sounding surprised.

"Don't look at me," Arrow said into the rearview mirror. "I don't have a cell phone."

"So you claim," Smollett replied.

"Perhaps Squire ditched it," Candy suggested.

The phone was still ringing. "I'll see who's calling." Smollett flicked on the phone, listened, then handed it to Arrow. "Some guy for you."

Arrow listened for several long moments, then

looked at us in the mirror. He was really upset. "There's terrible news. They need me in Coronach— Teresa has climbed the water tower. She's threatening to jump."

* * *

"But why?" I cried. "And what about Marie?"

"You'll never believe what happened! Marie and her grandmother ditched Teresa in Coronach. She was under treatment at the medical centre, and needed them, but they went home to Willow Bunch. Probably that's why she's threatening to jump—she feels betrayed. I can't understand Marie and Claire. It's not like them."

"How do you know it's true?"

Arrow nodded at the cell phone. "That was the doctor at the medical centre. I've got to save Teresa!" He looked at a collection of old buildings ahead. "I'll turn around at that abandoned ranch."

Most of the buildings had collapsed. Inside the shattered walls, I saw twisted timbers and weeds growing high. On the gate, a large sign said GILES RANCH. TRESPASSERS WILL BE GIVEN A FAIR TRIAL, THEN HUNG!

I looked at Candy. "That's not serious, is it?"

"I'm pretty sure it's a joke."

Arrow pulled the *Mañana Banana* into the road that led to the ranch. "You can't abandon us now," Smollett protested, as Arrow reversed the bus.

"I'm going to Coronach. You're welcome to come with me."

"But the sacred cat, man! There's money to be made."

"Teresa's life is what's important. Not money." Arrow looked at me. "You coming along?"

I shuddered. "No, I couldn't stand being in town. Not with Teresa doing that!" I looked at Candy. "Please, is it okay if I stay with you?"

"Of course."

Arrow opened the door. "Everyone off—quickly! I'll be back as soon as possible."

We pulled on jackets, and Smollett grabbed the flashlight as we climbed off the bus and watched the lights of the *Mañana Banana* disappear into the distance. Black clouds filled the sky. The wind was blowing hard, bending the few trees around us and swirling dust into our faces.

"What's with the weather?" I said nervously. "This is like starring in *The Wizard of Oz.*"

"A twister may be coming," Smollett replied. "Locals call it the Big Muddy Express."

"But twisters are dangerous!"

"If Big Muddy hits, we can take shelter in a cave. Now, let's get moving."

"Smollett's so weird," I whispered to Candy as we started walking. "He's consumed by greed. Suddenly, he's a different person."

"I don't trust Smollett—that's why I'm sticking close. Your aunt deserves a fair share of the reward if we find the cat. You and I will make sure Smollett doesn't cheat her."

"Okay!"

Around a bend, we entered a small valley. A stream

wandered through it. "Look," Candy said. "There's a beaver house."

"More caves! Some are at ground level."

Smollett pointed at a hill across the valley. "See the posts at the top? They mark the 49th parallel. Outlaws like Butch Cassidy and Sam Kelly escaped across the border on horseback and lived in these caves. It was perfect because the American sheriffs weren't allowed to cross the 49th to make an arrest."

"What about the North West Mounted Police?" I asked. "They could have arrested the outlaws north of the 49th parallel in Canadian territory."

"If a lookout spotted Mounties approaching, the outlaws left the caves and rode swiftly to the posts. By then, the American sheriffs would be long gone. Butch and Sam and their boys would watch from up the hill until the Red Coats moved on, then return to the caves."

"Those Mounties were stupid," Candy said. "They should have crossed the border and grabbed the outlaws. Nobody would have known."

"The officers would have known," Smollett sniffed. "Lawmen don't break the law. Only fools like Squire do that."

"I never trusted Squire," Candy said. "I've known liars and conmen, and he's one for sure."

Smollett nodded. "You're right, Candy. Squire does nothing but lie. He never once phoned the police. Not in Regina, not from Moose Jaw—never."

"How do you know?" I asked.

"Squire's been bragging to me. He can't keep a secret."

"But why didn't Squire phone the police?"

"He didn't want them learning about the disk. He'd have cheated us all."

We continued walking into the valley. Leaning close to Candy, I whispered, "Maybe Smollett deliberately got rid of Arrow. Do you think he sent a fake message about Teresa?"

"No." Candy's large green eyes glanced at me. "Only a very clever person would have tricked Arrow with a fake message. That's not Smollett's style. You're smart as paint, Liz, but he's not."

Then I heard a distant sound. "Listen! Isn't that a motorcycle?"

"I don't hear anything."

"I heard a roaring sound, but it must have been the storm."

The laptop's beeping grew louder as we approached a ground-level cave. Big boulders were scattered around. "I bet Sam Kelly lived in here," Smollett said to us. He sounded very excited. "Probably Butch Cassidy, too."

"I wonder if there's a grave here," I said, "like at the other coordinates."

"Could be," Smollett replied. "There are probably lots of ghosts floating around Big Muddy."

Gazing at the empty landscape, Candy shivered. "Brrr! This would be a horrible place to die."

The cave had a ragged opening shaped like a large doorway—a dark doorway. Smollett switched on the flashlight as we stepped inside. Dried mud surrounded us, and the air tasted of dirt. Wooden beams supported the roof. Strange shadows moved on the walls as Smollett flashed the light around until it stopped at a small, dark opening.

"That was their escape tunnel," he said. "It probably leads to a second cave, where the outlaws would have kept their horses."

"Why wouldn't they have kept their horses with them in this cave?" I said. "The entrance is big enough."

"Sure, but who'd live with horses?"

Candy looked around the cave with excited eyes. "The cat's here—I just know it. Please, let's find the statue!"

Smollett studied the wooden beams. "I bet it's hidden behind one of these." After exploring several beams, he grinned in triumph and produced a mud-smeared canvas bag. "I think I've found it."

*   *   *

Opening the bag, Smollett lifted out a golden statue— the Sacred Egyptian Cat! Set with precious stones that glittered in the flashlight's beam, the statue looked about 20 centimetres tall. "It's beautiful," I whispered. "Are those honestly real jewels?"

"You bet," Candy said. "Just look at the prisms of light flickering in the diamonds. What a sight!"

Around the cat's neck was a wide collar set with richly coloured gems; the flashlight reflected sparkles and twinkles from rubies, sapphires, and the amazing diamonds. Ears up, the cat was seated on its haunches, tail wrapped around its feet. It looked so dignified, yet so spectacular.

"This is solid gold," Candy breathed, taking the cat from Smollett. She gazed at the statue with reverence in her eyes. "You're more stunning than anyone could imagine, my beauty. It's so good to hold you at last."

"I don't see any pearls," I said. "That's good. Pearls mean tears are coming."

"I won't be crying." Smollett grabbed the cat from Candy. "I'm about to be a fabulously wealthy man," he told her. "Care to run away together?"

She shook her head. "No, thanks, Smollett. I've got standards."

"You're making a mistake, but it was worth a try." From his pocket, Smollett produced a small revolver. "I'll say goodbye. I'm leaving now with the Sacred Egyptian Cat. Don't try to stop me."

I was astonished. "Smollett, what are you doing? We're all supposed to share the reward."

"Sorry kid, but no chance. I'm escaping to the States. I'll melt down the statue, and sell the gold and jewels to crooked dealers for really big money. I'm glad I won. Squire's a sentimental fool. He would have returned the statue to Winter Leigh. That's what our arguments were about."

I expected Candy to be as terrified as I was, but she was perfectly calm. My eyes flicked around the cave, desperately searching the muddy grey walls for a way out. One hope was the escape tunnel, but it was beyond Smollett and he faced us with the revolver.

Then something amazing happened—out of the tunnel slithered a man carrying a coil of rope. He stood up, ready to attack Smollett. It was Tarantula!

* * *

For a brief moment, I stared in shock at the tattooed biker. Then Tarantula attacked, hitting Smollett from behind. Smollett went down hard, dropping the gun at Candy's feet. She looked at it, but made no move.

Pinning Smollett to the ground, Tarantula quickly roped his arms and legs. As he did, I watched Candy, wondering desperately why she didn't help.

Finally, Candy picked up the revolver. She looked at the gun, turning it slowly in her hand. I was amazed. She was acting like a zombie—she didn't seem to care about anything.

Staring at Candy with his horrible eyes, Tarantula slowly stood up from tying Smollett. "Candy," I cried. "Do something!"

"You're right, Liz, I should do something." With a smile on her face, Candy pointed the gun straight at me. "Maybe I should shoot you."

13

I was horrified. I stared at Candy, then Tarantula. They were grinning at each other. Quickly, I looked at Smollett, hoping somehow for help, but he'd been knocked out.

"Well, partner," Tarantula said, "the golden statue is ours."

I was unable to believe what was happening. "But," I finally stammered, "but . . ."

Grinning at me, Candy lifted off a black wig. Underneath was the short blonde hair of the biker who had shot Blind Pew. As I gasped in astonishment, Candy kissed the golden cat. "You're mine forever, my beauty. I've been heartsick with worry."

"What about Winter Leigh?" I said. "It's her property."

Candy's eyes blazed. "I hate that woman! As a kid, I lived in her Hollywood mansion—my parents were servants there. The Sacred Egyptian Cat was in a display case—I yearned for it, every day of my childhood. I wanted to hold the cat, but that cruel Winter Leigh would never let me."

I had a sudden thought. "I just figured something out. When you were sixteen, I bet you ran away with Billy Bones."

"That's right. We grew up together in Winter Leigh's mansion."

"But that means—Billy Bones was Winter Leigh's son!"

Candy nodded. "She was kind to Billy, but he was always angry at life. As for me, I was just plain bored. So, on my sixteenth birthday, I convinced Billy to run away with me. For a few years, it was okay. Then we fell in with a biker gang."

"The Death Machine?"

"Yes. It wasn't long before I got sick of Billy, and became Blind Pew's old lady. He was a real tough guy. Everyone feared Pew. He'd lost his eyes in biker warfare, but still controlled the Death Machine."

"Until you killed him!"

Candy shrugged. "Billy was miserable when I was with Pew, but he stayed with the Death Machine. Then he got into drugs big time, and desperately needed money. He agreed to steal his mother's golden statue for me."

"Why did you need Billy's help? Why didn't you just steal it yourself?"

"The Sacred Egyptian Cat was protected by a computer alarm system that was impossible to beat." Candy smiled. "But the system had been designed by Billy himself—he'd always been a computer genius."

"So he broke into his mother's mansion, and stole the cat?"

Candy nodded. "The night it happened, I was waiting outside the mansion, but Billy betrayed me. He escaped with *my* cat!"

"Why'd he go to Saskatchewan? That's a long journey."

"I'm sure Billy couldn't decide what to do about the cat. He needed to hide it—to give him time to think. As kids, Billy and his sister explored Big Muddy while their mom was making a movie here. He was always telling me about the caves, and what a great hiding place they'd make." Candy smiled. "So I figured Billy would head north with the cat, and I was right."

"You convinced the Death Machine to help you find him?"

"That's right," Candy replied. "I told them we'd melt down the statue, and share a fortune. Of course, I was lying about my intentions." She kissed the statue's golden head. "We tracked Billy to an abandoned farm, but he escaped. After we lost him, we went back and trashed the farm, looking for the cat, but Billy had hidden it somewhere."

"Why didn't he escape from you on his motorcycle?"

"We closed in fast—he didn't get a chance. Billy had a book with him, so I figured something was inside it, maybe a computer disk that would lead me to the cat. But when we found Billy dead at Benbow Farm, the book was missing."

"I had it."

"That's what I guessed. At the farm, I saw Squire's address on the fax machine, so we headed for Regina. I got into his house and was searching for the book when you came home. I was watching from upstairs when you found the disk."

"You were the person who jumped me?"

"That's right—I was hoping to get the disk. Then I realized it didn't matter. From what I'd heard in hiding, you alone knew the password. Besides, Squire was a computer brain who could save me the trouble of finding the cat. I decided to join the expedition, and go along for the ride until he found the cat. Then I'd kill Squire and take it."

"And kill the rest of us?" I said indignantly.

Candy shrugged. "Hopefully, no."

"You're horrible! I can't believe I liked you."

She ignored my outburst. "Since Squire had talked about hiring Arrow's bus, I decided to replace Teresa as cook for the treasure hunt. That's why we kidnapped her, so Arrow would need a replacement cook for the expedition—and I'd be that cook."

"You lied to everyone, Candy. You even convinced Arrow to believe that Teresa had abandoned him."

She nodded. "I couldn't risk his helping Marie to find Teresa—too much could have gone wrong."

"So you never fell for Arrow?"

"I didn't say that, Liz." Candy's green eyes were sad. "Arrow's a wonderful guy, and they're lucky to have each other."

"So Teresa was kidnapped after leaving the bar in Regina?"

Tarantula grinned at me with jagged teeth. "Yes— we talked to Teresa at the bar, to be sure she was the right person. Then we took her hostage. Candy wrote a note in lipstick, and left it for Arrow to find."

"I'd seen the IMAX tickets on Squire's desk," Candy explained, "so it was easy to meet you and Melody and gain your trust. The Death Machine trailed our expedition to Moose Jaw, and holed up in the garage. I wanted them around as backup when the Egyptian cat was located."

I looked at Tarantula. "We almost caught you in Moose Jaw when you arrived at the restaurant to meet Candy."

"So big deal already," he sneered. "I got away."

"You girls worried me that evening," Candy said. "You were getting close to the truth. I left the restaurant real fast for the garage. I wanted the Death Machine out of Moose Jaw before any cops showed up."

"We saw you through the wall. But we didn't recognize you without the wig."

"I had to disguise myself, in case you'd seen me at Benbow Farm. The wig was inside my tote bag at the garage."

I thought back to that night. "Remember when we returned to the motel? I noticed that your black hair was a mess. I guess that's because you'd pulled on the wig in a hurry."

Candy turned to Tarantula with a dirty look. "You fools went to Gravelbourg, instead of Assiniboia, as I ordered."

"I already told you, Candy, those Moose Jaw bikers

suggested the bishop's house would be a perfect hide-out. They were right. We kept the bikes in the garage, and Teresa in the attic. It was excellent."

"Sure," Candy said sarcastically, "but what about Sister Rita? When you took her from Gravelbourg as a hostage, you forgot her medication. Returning to the bishop's house for it delayed the operation."

Tarantula stared at the muddy ground, saying nothing.

I looked at Candy. "Did you and Tarantula use cell phones to communicate? I never saw you with one."

"Mine's miniaturized. I kept it in my backpack." She paused, thinking. "Smollett had given me his business card. I called his office with a message that Smollett was needed in Gravelbourg. Then I sabotaged the *Banana* to guarantee enough time to discuss strategy with Tarantula at the cathedral. We were in the office when you girls showed up. I ordered Sister Rita to get rid of you."

"The nun knew too much," Tarantula said. "I made her write a note saying she'd gone to a sick relative in Regina, and she became our second hostage."

"When Sister Rita was praying at the altar," I said to Candy, "you beckoned from the shadows, didn't you? I saw a flash of red—it must have been your ruby ring."

Tarantula looked at me. "After Gravelbourg, we hid at an abandoned farm. When Sister Rita needed her medication, I used the cell phone to request another day's delay."

"I sabotaged the bus again at Willow Bunch," Candy explained. "Then I heard you girls discussing Tarantula's message."

"Marie had a scanner," I said.

"So I figured. Instead of risking the cell phone, I signalled Tarantula we'd be going to Coronach."

"I saw your Morse code."

"I gave you a good scare in the museum," Candy said with satisfaction. "I hope it taught you a lesson: Don't be snoopy, or you'll die."

I didn't think she'd shoot me, but I wasn't so sure about Tarantula. Looking at the gun, I wondered how to get it from Candy. I was really scared, but I had to stall for time. "Did you steal the key for the handcuffs from my backpack and slip it to Tarantula?"

Candy nodded. "Then, at the Marshall grave, I learned the final coordinates. I wanted Tarantula to know them, so he could continue to follow us. I took a chance and phoned him from the WC on the bus. Then I wrapped my cell phone in a towel and dropped it into the laundry hamper, knowing Tarantula would be calling Arrow with a fake message from a fake doctor saying Teresa was in peril."

"She was never planning to jump from the water tower?"

"Of course not," Candy replied. "Teresa's safe and sound in Coronach, along with the others. Too bad you're not with them, Liz. You should have returned to Coronach with Squire in that pickup truck."

"You wouldn't kill me, Candy. You're not the kind."

"Actually, you're right—I'd never hurt a kid. However, I could use a hostage and that hostage is you."

I looked outside. The black sky was lit by flashes of approaching lightning, and the wind moaned past the cave. "Let's wait until this storm's over, okay? It looks dangerous out there."

As Candy hesitated, I quickly added, "One thing I can't figure. Why did Billy Bones create such an elaborate route to the sacred cat?"

"He had to allow for the possibility of someone stealing the disk. You saw how it took forever to find our way here. I guess Billy figured that if someone stole the disk, he could head straight to Big Muddy and grab the cat first."

"Just before he died, Billy Bones gave me his book. He wanted me to find someone—I guess it was Winter Leigh."

Candy nodded. "Billy always loved his mother. He knew the statue was her dearest possession, and he hated the thought of stealing it. Billy had a weak heart and always feared dying—I'm sure he planned to send the disk to Winter Leigh. That way, she could find the cat if he died."

Smollett groaned—he was slowly coming around. Then Tarantula spat on the ground. "Come on, Candy, let's get moving. Bad weather's rising—it's as dark out there as the inside of a cow."

"First, give me your gun."

Reaching inside his leather jacket, Tarantula handed Candy a small, black pistol.

"You made some dumb mistakes, Tarantula, especially when you let the others return to California. I don't like that." Candy stared at the biker for a moment, then handed him a small, round piece of paper.

"The Black Spot," Tarantula groaned. "Please, Candy, no!"

"Yes." Her voice was cold. "Dead men tell no tales. It's goodbye, Tarantula."

As she levelled the revolver at him, I cried, "Candy, don't—it would be horrible!"

She looked at me, then slowly lowered the gun. "You're a nice kid, Liz, so I'll grant you the favour. Tarantula doesn't die." She pointed at the handcuffs dangling from his leather belt. "Grab those."

Quickly, I did as she ordered.

"Cuff Tarantula's wrist to Smollett's ankle. Hurry!"

Both men protested, but Candy had the guns. As the cuffs snapped closed, she emptied the bullets out of Tarantula's pistol and threw the pistol out of the cave. Then she kissed the Sacred Egyptian Cat. "I'm taking this beauty home across the border, and we're leaving now. I'm sure Tarantula's Harley is close by."

Stepping from the cave, we were blasted by the wind. Behind the dark clouds, lightning exploded in white flashes. It was scary to see. Tarantula's motorcycle was nearby—Candy pushed me towards it with the gun. "Let's go!" she yelled into the wind.

As lightning flashed, I saw a woollen sash stretched between two boulders at ankle level. Stepping over the sash, I distracted Candy by pointing at the sky. "Oh no! Is that a funnel cloud?"

Candy looked up. "I don't see one. Just keep—"

At that moment, Candy tripped over the sash. As she fell with a shout of surprise, Marie leapt from hiding. "Quickly, Liz," she cried. "We can escape on Sundance!"

"I'm so glad to see you," I yelled, as we raced together to her horse. "Is your mom okay?"

"Yes!"

"How'd you get here?"

"I saw Arrow in town. He said he'd left you at the Giles Ranch. Liz, I was so worried for you. I took off on Sundance, just in case you needed help. I've made the ride before. From the ranch, I tracked you to the cave." She watched Candy at the motorcycle, securing the statue in a saddlebag. "Where's her gun?"

"In my hand." I showed Marie the revolver. "Candy dropped it when your sash tripped her."

"Good work, Liz!"

The roar of the bike's engine rose on the wind. Headlight glaring, the Harley turned into the darkness. "Climb up, Liz," Marie said, pulling me onto Sundance.

Arms around her waist, I looked at the motorcycle bouncing and weaving across the valley. "Candy's got the Sacred Egyptian Cat."

"Wow!"

"If only we could get it back, Marie. The statue is so important to Winter Leigh."

"That's rough terrain Candy is trying to cross. It'll slow her down, and Sundance is really fast. Maybe we can catch up to Candy."

"Okay, let's try!"

Sundance waded through the shallow stream and began galloping across the valley. She was surefooted and strong, and quickly brought us closer to Candy as the Harley reached the hill and roared up, making for the border.

The rain came suddenly, lashing down in wet sheets. Thunder crashed above our heads. The Harley's wheels began to slip, but Candy forced it on, and she reached the hilltop before us. By the time we got there, the Harley was stopped just beyond the posts that marked the 49th parallel. As we came close to Candy, she grinned at us.

"I'm back in the U.S.A.!" Opening the saddlebag, Candy raised the Sacred Egyptian Cat in triumph. "Victory is mine," she cried over the roaring thunder. "I'm smarter than anyone!"

"We've got the gun," I yelled. "You're under arrest."

"You've got to be kidding, Liz." Candy secured the golden statue in the saddlebag. "You couldn't shoot me, and besides—you're a Canadian. You'd have to cross the border illegally to make the arrest, and you'd never do that."

I looked past Candy into Montana. The rugged land was similar to Saskatchewan, and so was the weather. It was vicious. Lightning flashed constantly behind menacing clouds, and the wind roared and shrieked, shaking us with its power.

But that wasn't all.

In the distance, a twirling grey funnel was moving rapidly our way. "Holy Hannah," I cried. "That must be the twister they call Big Muddy!"

* * *

I looked across the border at Candy, lit vividly by flashes of white light. Like us, she'd been soaked by the torrential rain. "Come back to the cave," I shouted to her. "It's the only shelter from the twister!"

"Not a chance." Candy powered up the Harley. "I can outrun anything." For a moment, she gazed at us. "You're smart kids. Too bad you're honest—we'd have made a great team." She waved goodbye, then headed south. Watching her go, I felt a curious sadness. Then I stared at the twister.

"Come on, Marie," I yelled above the howling gale. "Let's move it!"

The incredible wind was tossing tumbleweeds and all kinds of junk through the air. Sundance had difficulty finding her way down the slippery hillside, but we reached the valley safely. As our brave horse galloped towards the cave, I looked over my shoulder—the twister was close behind, spreading a cloud of dust and dirt across the land. Branches and bits of wood and dozens of tumbleweeds swirled through the air. I couldn't believe the noise—it was horrifying.

"Faster, Sundance," Marie cried in great fear. "Hurry, hurry!"

The cave was straight ahead. We jumped down from Sundance, and quickly led her inside—the horse needed no coaxing. Tarantula and Smollett were still there, cuffed together. They looked very scared.

"Is that a twister I hear?" Smollett cried. "Is it Big Muddy?"

"Yes!" I replied.

"What about Candy?" Tarantula demanded.

"She escaped."

"From Big Muddy?" Smollett said. "Not necessarily."

At that moment, the twister hit. Marie and I hugged each other, terrified, as we listened to a noise like a million explosions. White light flashed, flashed, flashed outside the cave while we shrieked in terror—and then suddenly the twister was gone. A final, moaning cry came from the winds before they grew silent, and the danger became only a memory.

Marie led Sundance outside, and I followed. In the distance, lightning flashed silently in the dark sky; up close, the wet ground was littered with tree branches, tumbleweeds, and rubble. Marie found us blankets in the saddlebags, then began towelling down her horse. "My hero," I said, stroking Sundance's face. "You saved our lives."

The *Mañana Banana* appeared around a corner. Arrow jumped out and ran our way. With him were Aunt Melody and Teresa, who hugged us and cried. When we finally stopped blubbering, I turned towards Arrow and got a real shock. In his hand was the Sacred Egyptian Cat.

* * *

"Candy is dead," Arrow said. "We found her near the Giles Ranch. The motorcycle is there, too. It's a mess."

I looked at Marie. "The twister got her."

"The ranch was totalled," Teresa said. "Melody found the Egyptian cat in a saddlebag. A couple of gems are loose, but otherwise it seems okay."

"Winter Leigh will be really happy," Marie said.

"Was Candy secretly one of the bikers?" Aunt Melody asked. "That's what we figured, when we found her next to the Harley."

"Yes," I replied. "She betrayed us."

After hearing the details, Aunt Melody said, "Poor Candy—what a tragedy. But she was right about one thing. She didn't die from smoking."

"I'm going to miss her," I said. "Was Coronach hit by the twister?"

"Happily, no."

Eventually, the Mounties arrived and began an investigation. After Marie and I had given statements, we loaded Sundance into a horse trailer brought to the scene by Lily. After that, we climbed into Lily's pickup and headed for Coronach. Thinking about Candy's unhappy death, I shed a tear for her. Then I looked at Marie. What an adventure we had shared!

* * *

Soon after, a celebration was held at Lily's farm. Neighbours brought fresh bread and doughnuts and cold roasts and pies and tarts, but the biggest hit was Teresa's bannock. The bread was so crisp and sugary—my stomach was bulging! People stood around the table in the big kitchen, eating heartily as they discussed the safe return of the Sacred Egyptian Cat to its home in Hollywood with Winter Leigh.

Special guests at the event were George and Doris Husband, who'd driven all the way from Benbow Farm. "Our house has been repaired," Doris told us, "and our neighbours arranged an old-fashioned barn-raising."

George nodded. "They built us a brand-new barn. It's a wonderful gift." He smiled at me. "You and your aunt must return next summer. After all, you didn't get to ride our horses."

"That sounds great!"

Arrow and Teresa strolled into the kitchen. They

were holding hands. "When I thought Teresa was threatening to jump," Arrow told me, "I was desperately frightened." He looked at her. "When I reached Coronach and learned the message was a fake, I broke down and cried. I've never felt so happy."

"That makes me feel better," I said. "During the trip I worried you'd fallen for Candy."

"Not a chance—kissing a smoker is like kissing an ashtray. Besides, I never trusted that woman. I followed Candy a couple of times, trying to figure out her game, but I didn't learn anything. I guess I'm no Sherlock Holmes."

"I made mistakes myself," I said. "I never thought Candy was wearing a wig, even when she wouldn't let Aunt Melody style her hair. Not only that, but when we talked at Mac the Moose, she said the bikers were American. How could she have known that?"

"Candy was supposed to be from Moose Jaw," Marie pointed out, "but she didn't know Gravelbourg is a French community. Everyone around here knows that."

"She even referred to the cross-Canada highway, but we all know it's the Trans-Canada." I thought about seeing Candy at Benbow Farm, when she'd shot Blind Pew. "As a biker, she had a bunch of earrings and studs. When we first met Candy, at the IMAX theatre, I noticed her ears had been pierced, but I didn't make the connection."

I turned to Marie. "Remember showing Candy the picture of your mom? She commented that Teresa looked better with red hair. That was a clue I missed."

"You're still a great detective," Marie said. "I predict a brilliant future in sleuthing."

"I agree," Teresa said, and the others all nodded. Teresa then handed me a present; it was a dream catcher fashioned with splendid feathers. "I made this especially for you, Liz. Thank you for believing in Marie, and helping her find me."

"It's beautiful, Teresa! What a perfect souvenir of my very first detective case."

Marie turned to her mother. "You know the reward Winter Leigh is sending us for finding the cat? With some of my share, I want to finance your first video. We can send it to Country Music Television, and you'll become a star."

"Oh, sweetheart, that's so kind of you."

"I'm really proud of you, Mom. You're a great singer."

I looked at Arrow—he was smiling. "Give it a try, Teresa. If it will make you happy."

Aunt Melody turned to me and Marie. "I'm so impressed with you girls. When I'm an opera singer, I'll dedicate my first performance especially to you."

* * *

Liz looks at the image of Alice on her Liquid\Screen. "You've heard of the Hollywood Bowl? People listen to music under the stars; it's very romantic. Aunt Melody's first professional singing engagement was at the Bowl, and I was in the audience with Marie."

"Did you get to meet Winter Leigh?"

"Oh yes. We were invited to her mansion. She was very glamorous. When I saw the Sacred Egyptian Cat in its display case, I thought of Candy as a little girl,

gazing at the beautiful cat she could never hold. The hungers of the human heart can be so sad."

Liz switches on the News Channel. "Excuse me for a moment, Alice. The SuperBrain-987 computer will have calculated the results by now."

The numbers scroll rapidly across the screen: the vote has passed by a majority of many millions. "Excellent," Liz says. "Canadians have decided against commercial use of our parklands. That's what I wanted."

"On the School Channel, we studied the origins of computer democracy. I was amazed to learn that, in earlier times, Canadians only got to vote every few years."

Alice looks at the notes she's been making about Liz Austen's first case. "Did Teresa and Arrow stay together?"

Liz nods. "The video that Marie financed was a major hit. Teresa had gigs all over the world—she even sang for King William! But eventually she got tired of it all. She settled down with Arrow on a farm near Willow Bunch, having kids and raising organic vegetables to sell."

"Tarantula went to prison?"

Liz nods.

"What happened to Smollett?"

"He was in big trouble for carrying a weapon. The last I heard, Smollett and Squire were living in the same seniors' residence. They were still bickering."

"And Marie?"

"That's the best of all. She's devoted her life to the Métis. Recently, she received their highest honour, the

Order of the Sash." Tears of pride fill Liz's eyes. "It couldn't have happened to a finer person."

"Hey, look at the time. It's getting late."

"How's the mystery you're writing, Alice?"

"It's coming along nicely, thanks."

"Remember what I said—keep it short. You're still too young to write a book-length story."

"I've been thinking, Liz. Your Big Muddy adventure reminded me a lot of Treasure Island."

"You're right! I guess there'll always be stories to tell of fabulous treasures, and mysterious strangers like Billy Bones."

Alice looks at Liz with affection. "I'd better go. Goodnight, Liz. Thanks for the story."

"It was fun, Alice. We'll talk again."

Eric Wilson at Big Muddy

WILLIE AND TILLIE DUNCAN

Reading *Treasure Island* sent shivers through Eric Wilson when he was a boy. Eric's mystery *Escape from Big Muddy* was written as a tribute to Robert Louis Stevenson, the author of *Treasure Island*. If you read Stevenson's tale, or watch it on video, you'll enjoy finding parallels between the two stories (for example, how both Jim Hawkins and Liz Austen witness important plot events from the inside of an apple barrel). Eric hopes that—many years in the future— another adventure author will take up the challenge to again retell *Treasure Island*.

Because his dad was a Mountie, Eric Wilson enjoyed researching the RCMP for this book. He was also interested in the story of Louis Riel and the Métis people, and other aspects of Saskatchewan history. In this mystery, Eric once again uses real settings as the backdrop to his story. Perhaps one day you'll explore these scenes yourself!

THE ICE DIAMOND QUEST

A Tom and Liz Austen Mystery

ERIC WILSON

The yacht, driven by its power, was closing in fast. Ahead, the sea roared against a low reef, throwing white water into the dark night.

Why is a mysterious yacht flashing a signal off the coast of Newfoundland on a cold November evening? Tom and Liz Austen, with their cousins Sarah and Duncan Joy, follow a difficult trail toward the truth. As they search, someone called the Hawk and people known as the Renegades cause major problems, but the cousins press on. In the darkness of an abandoned mine and later on stormy seas, they face together the greatest dangers ever.

"I read *The Ice Diamond Quest* and now I'm hooked on books."

—*Tamara K., Lachine, Québec*

SPIRIT IN THE RAINFOREST

A Tom and Liz Austen Mystery

ERIC WILSON

The branches trembled, then something slipped away into the darkness of the forest. "That was Mosquito Joe!" Tom exclaimed.

"Or his spirit," Liz said. "Let's get out of here."

The rainforest of British Columbia holds many secrets, but none stranger than those of Nearby Island. After hair-raising events during a Pacific storm, Tom and Liz Austen seek answers among the island's looming trees. Alarmed by the ghostly shape of the hermit Mosquito Joe, they look for shelter in a deserted school in the rainforest. Then, in the night, Tom and Liz hear a girl's voice crying, *"Beware! Beware!"*

"My family was surprised I was reading, but I love this book. It was inspiring and interesting, and I highly recommend that other kids read it."

—*Krystle T., LeFory, Ontario*

THE INUK MOUNTIE ADVENTURE

A Tom Austen Mystery

ERIC WILSON

Out on the frozen sea, they stopped to look at Gjoa Haven. The houses of the tiny hamlet seemed defenceless, huddled together under the roaring flames. Sam shook his head. "What a disaster for these good people."

What is the sinister conspiracy code-named CanSell, and how does it threaten Canada? Is the nation's handsome Prime Minister really what he seems? The truth is on a micro-cassette that Tom Austen must somehow find before a crucial vote by Canadians on the future of the country.

While on a school trip to Gjoa Haven in the high Arctic, Tom unexpectedly learns the cassette might be closer than he thought. Between drum dances and snow-mobile chases across the tundra, Tom searches for the cassette and learns a valuable lesson from the Inuit about the futility of violence.

"I totally freak out when I find an Eric Wilson book I haven't read yet."

—*Danica J., Yellowknife, NWT*

"This story was full of action and suspense. I thought it written well and with good taste."

—*Ian K., Toronto, Ontario*

SUMMER OF DISCOVERY

ERIC WILSON

As his pulse raced, Ian sat staring at the piano—feeling terribly afraid and terribly excited.

Do ghosts of hymn-singing children haunt a cluster of abandoned buildings on the Saskatchewan prairie? The story of how the kids from Terry Fox Cabin answer that question will thrill you from page one of this exciting book. Eric Wilson, author of many fast-moving mysteries, presents here a tale of adventure, humour and the triumph of the human spirit.

"It was great! I liked how Ian slowly got over his fears and was ready to admit to them."

—*Matthew B., Winnipeg, Manitoba*

THE UNMASKING OF 'KSAN

ERIC WILSON

Spray billowed into the air and I could hear a roaring that rapidly grew louder.

"Rapids!" I screamed. "Straight ahead!"

The theft of a valuable mask brings sorrow to Dawn's people. Determined to recover it, she turns to Graham for help and together they begin a search that plunges them into suspense and danger. The rugged mountains and surging rivers of northern British Columbia are the backdrop to an adventure you will never forget.

"I liked the characters a lot and I think Eric Wilson should write another book about Graham and Dawn."
—*Seth P., Grand Forks, British Columbia*